LET IT BE KNOWN that passionate
Princess Elizabeth fell for her noble lover,
identity unknown. But this strong-willed
woman refused to settle for shotgun
vows to secure her secret baby's
legitimacy. She wanted the fairy tale....

LET IT BE KNOWN that heir-apparent-
turned-apparent-construction-company-CEO
Raphael "Rafe" Thorton has claimed the
remaining Wynborough princess as his bride,
solidifying the relationship between the two
island nations...and perhaps mending his own
relationship with his dad, the Grand Duke?

All of Wynborough—and Thortonburg—
celebrate these latest nuptials. But what's this
we hear about a shocking royal revelation...?

• • • • • • • • • • • • •

Don't miss *Man...Mercenary...Monarch*,
the exciting finale of ROYALLY WED,
available next month in Silhouette Special Edition.

Dear Reader,

Please join us in celebrating Silhouette's 20th anniversary in 2000! We promise to deliver—all year—passionate, powerful, provocative love stories from your favorite Desire authors!

This January, look for bestselling author Leanne Banks's first MAN OF THE MONTH with *Her Forever Man*. Watch sparks fly when irresistibly rugged ranch owner Brock Logan comes face-to-face with his new partner, the fiery Felicity Chambeau, in the first book of Leanne's brand-new miniseries LONE STAR FAMILIES: THE LOGANS.

Desire is pleased to continue the Silhouette cross-line continuity ROYALLY WED with *The Pregnant Princess* by favorite author Anne Marie Winston. After a night of torrid passion with a stranger, a beautiful princess ends up pregnant...and seeks out the father of her child.

Elizabeth Bevarly returns to Desire with her immensely popular miniseries FROM HERE TO MATERNITY with *Dr. Mommy,* about a couple reunited by a baby left on a doorstep. *Hard Lovin' Man,* another of Peggy Moreland's TEXAS BRIDES, captures the intensity of falling in love when a cowgirl gives her heart to a sweet-talkin', hard-lovin' hunk. Cathleen Galitz delivers a compelling marriage-of-convenience tale in *The Cowboy Takes a Bride,* in the series THE BRIDAL BID. And Sheri WhiteFeather offers another provocative Native American hero in *Skyler Hawk: Lone Brave.*

Help us celebrate 20 years of great romantic fiction from Silhouette by indulging yourself with all six delectably sensual Desire titles each and every month during this special year!

Enjoy!

Joan Marlow Golan
Senior Editor, Silhouette Desire

Please address questions and book requests to:
Silhouette Reader Service
U.S.: 3010 Walden Ave., P.O. Box 1325, Buffalo, NY 14269
Canadian: P.O. Box 609, Fort Erie, Ont. L2A 5X3

The Pregnant Princess

ANNE MARIE WINSTON

Silhouette® Desire

Published by Silhouette Books

America's Publisher of Contemporary Romance

Special thanks and acknowledgment are given
to Anne Marie Winston for her contribution to
the *Royally Wed* series.

For Sandy,
sister of my heart

SILHOUETTE BOOKS

ISBN 0-373-76268-2

THE PREGNANT PRINCESS

Copyright © 2000 by Harlequin Books S.A.

Visit us at www.romance.net

Printed in U.S.A.

Books by Anne Marie Winston

Silhouette Desire

Best Kept Secrets #742
Island Baby #770
Chance at a Lifetime #809
Unlikely Eden #827
Carolina on My Mind #845
Substitute Wife #863
Find Her, Keep Her #887
Rancher's Wife #936
Rancher's Baby #1031
Seducing the Proper Miss Miller #1155
The Baby Consultant #1191
Dedicated to Deirdre #1197
The Bride Means Business #1204
Lovers' Reunion #1226
The Pregnant Princess #1268

*Butler County Brides

ANNE MARIE WINSTON

has believed in happy endings all her life. Having the opportunity to share them with her readers gives her great joy. Anne Marie enjoys figure skating and working in the gardens of her south-central Pennsylvania home.

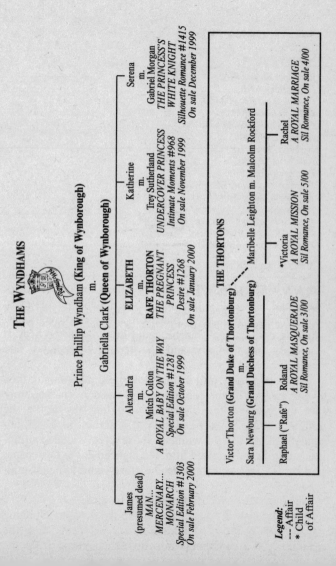

THE WYNDHAMS

Prince Phillip Wyndham (King of Wynborough)
m.
Gabriella Clark (Queen of Wynborough)

James (presumed dead)
MAN... MERCENARY... MONARCH
Special Edition #1303
On sale February 2000.

Alexandra
m.
Mitch Colton
A ROYAL BABY ON THE WAY
Special Edition #1281
On sale October 1999

ELIZABETH
m.
RAFE THORTON
THE PREGNANT PRINCESS
Desire #1268
On sale January 2000

Katherine
m.
Trey Sutherland
UNDERCOVER PRINCESS
Intimate Moments #968
On sale November 1999

Serena
m.
Gabriel Morgan
THE PRINCESS'S WHITE KNIGHT
Silhouette Romance #1415
On sale December 1999

THE THORTONS

Victor Thorton (Grand Duke of Thortonburg)
m.
Sara Newburg (Grand Duchess of Thortonburg)

- - - - Maribelle Leighton m. Malcolm Rockford

Raphael ("Rafe")
A ROYAL MASQUERADE
Sil Romance, On sale 3/00

Roland
A ROYAL MASQUERADE
Sil Romance, On sale 3/00

*Victoria
A ROYAL MISSION
Sil Romance, On sale 5/00

Rachel
A ROYAL MARRIAGE
Sil Romance, On sale 4/00

Legend:
- - - - Affair
* Child of Affair

One

God, it was hot. Rafe Thorton ran a hand through his thick black hair and pulled his sunglasses down over his eyes. Arizona might be a great place for a guy employed year-round in construction, but he could do without the heat. It was only late January and the temperature today had reached the mid-eighties.

Rafe took a long pull of the water he'd just bought, then swung away from the cool interior of the convenience store into the heat of the afternoon. Juggling the bottle, he stripped off his T-shirt and swiped it across his chest, absently smiling at two women whose eyes widened in appreciation as they passed him. He glanced at the newspaper box on the sidewalk outside the store—and stopped mid-stride.

Wynborough Princess Dedicates Hospice.

Rafe stared at the headlines of the daily paper. Slinging the T-shirt over one shoulder, he set his drink atop the machine for a moment while he fished coins from the pocket of his faded jeans. He dropped a quarter and a dime through the slot, then opened the door and pulled out a paper.

Wynborough was a tiny kingdom; its royalty rarely received the kind of press that Britain's royals were subjected to regularly. There was a brief press release accompanied by one small candid photo, a blurry shot of a small, slender woman stepping out of a car.

Holding the paper close to his face as if that might bring it into better focus, he stared at the grainy picture. The woman's hair obscured much of her face and he couldn't discern its color from the black-and-white shot. Still...it could be her.

The features that had consumed his dreams for the past five months floated before his mind's eye as he scanned the article. Memories bombarded him, and his pulse sped up. Princess Elizabeth would be arriving in Phoenix, Arizona, this afternoon. She'd be staying for several days, making an appearance tomorrow to raise funds for a local children's hospice.

Elizabeth! Was that *her* name?

He tossed the paper across the seat as he climbed into his truck and started the engine. Wynborough. Five months before, he'd attended one of the royal charity events, a masquerade ball. It had been the first time he'd been home in ten years, the first time since the day he'd informed his father, the Grand Duke of Thortonburg, that he had no intention of assuming the title or of living under his father's thumb. And hearing himself addressed as the Prince of Thortonburg by his family's servants, the title that had descended onto his shoulders along with all the other responsibilities he'd been trained to handle all his life, had reminded him forcibly of all the reasons why he'd made the decision to live in the States.

He didn't want those responsibilities.

Wryly, he wondered what his father, who'd harped on

responsibility all his life, would think if he knew Rafe had seduced one of the Wynborough princesses in a garden house five months ago. Not a very *responsible* act, even if the lady had been as hot and ready as he had been.

He'd thought about her a great deal since then. She'd been gentle and sweet, with a hint of innocence that had turned out to be more than a hint. But she'd been so warm and willing that he'd found himself unable to resist her, even though he had better sense. At least he'd told her right up front that he would be leaving the next morning, he thought. She couldn't accuse him of not being honest about his intentions.

But that was a moot point. He hadn't told her who he was, and he had never expected to see his pretty lover again. He just hadn't anticipated that she'd be so deeply embedded in his memory that he caught himself thinking of her at all hours of the day and night.

Yes, he'd thought about her far too much.

Irritably, Rafe drummed his fingers on the steering wheel, waiting for the light to change. Although he couldn't imagine that she'd known who he was, years of thwarting his father's machinations had honed his suspicious nature. His mouth tightened. Did he discern his father's match-making hand in the princess's sudden appearance in Phoenix? Had the old man found out somehow about that night?

He felt his shoulders tensing and he took a deep breath, forcing himself to relax. Maybe it was simple coincidence. Maybe it wasn't even the right princess, if indeed his mystery lover had been one of the Wynborough princesses.

Then again, maybe years of living away had dulled his instinct for self-preservation. His father had an incredible capacity for trying to force the issue of a royal marriage on his firstborn son. If he'd even heard any of Rafe's firm denials, there certainly was no evidence of it.

But he didn't intend to marry anybody with royal blood. Ever. Being heir to the damned title his family so revered had caused him more grief in his childhood than any kid should have had to bear. He had no intention of foisting it onto any offspring of his own. No, the Duchy of Thortonburg would pass to his younger brother Roland.

As for marriage…when and if he ever felt the time was right, he planned to find a nice American girl of common ancestry and settle down in anonymous wedded bliss.

No way was he marrying a princess!

He picked up the discarded paper and read the article again. She was staying at the newly opened Shalimar Resort. Now that was handy. His company had gotten the bid to complete work in a courtyard at the Shalimar, and he still had a crew there. Maybe he'd run by there right now and see how the work was progressing.

It was a lovely hotel, Elizabeth thought, admiring the muted dusty rose and pale marble colors of Phoenix's newest five-star resort. But then, she was used to lovely things. What she wasn't used to was freedom.

She supposed to most of the people milling around in the lobby as she moved toward the restaurant, walking alone through a five-star hotel was so ordinary as to be forgettable. But to her, accustomed as she was to bodyguards and security systems, schedules and surveillance cameras, it was incredibly exciting. Daring.

A little scary.

"Ma'am, do you have a reservation?" the maitre d' asked as she approached.

She smiled. "Yes. Elizabeth Wyndham. One for dinner."

Instantly, the man's inquiring expression changed to one of delight. "Ah, Princess Elizabeth! Your Royal Highness, may I welcome you to La Belle Maison. Your table has been prepared." He bowed low and gestured for her to precede him, pointing to a candlelit alcove where a server stood with napkins at the ready.

Elizabeth took the seat they had prepared, allowing the men to fuss over her every comfort, refusing wine and asking for a menu. But as she perused the selections, her mind was still out in the lobby, where for a few minutes she'd walked alone, free, with no one to worship her, no one to worry about every step she took or every person she passed.

She sighed. "I'll have the special, a salad with your house dressing, and the carrots. No potato, thank you."

As the waiter rushed off, she felt a slight but very real movement pushing at the wall of her womb. Discreetly covering her abdomen with one hand, she patted the small bulge beneath her fashionably loose-fitting pants and tunic top. *Hello, my sweet one. Perhaps we'll meet your daddy today.*

She rested her chin on one hand. Oh, how she hoped she'd be able to find the mysterious man with whom she'd shared such a wonderful night of loving five months ago. He'd said he was American, though he'd sounded as if he'd been a native of her father's kingdom. And though he'd had to return to the States, he'd left behind his card—a clue—letting her know where she could find him.

Thorton Design and Construction, Phoenix, Arizona. U.S.A. Apparently her baby's father worked for the firm.

She'd hoped he would come back for her and, of course, that was still possible. In fact, she was sure he would, since she was absolutely positive he had felt the extraordinary bond between them as strongly as she had.

But she couldn't wait much longer. He didn't know she was on a rather urgent schedule now. Her spirits took a mild plunge. Soon she was going to have to tell her parents about her pregnancy. It was becoming difficult to hide it with clothing. When she'd had the opportunity to come to the States with her three sisters to search for their long-lost brother, she'd seized the chance, hoping for the opportunity to slip away and seek out her mystery lover.

It had been the sheerest good fortune that their search

had led them to Hope, Arizona, to a foster home where their kidnapped brother might have been brought nearly thirty years ago. And even better fortune that Catalina, where she was going to interview a man who might be that brother, was but a few hours' drive from her current location, providing her with a perfectly good reason to stay in Phoenix.

Arranging a charity event for the hospice project had been easy. Now she could only hope that the excuse the event had given her to visit Phoenix brought back into her life her Prince Charming from the charity ball.

Oh, he'd been so handsome, so wonderful. From the moment their eyes had met across the crowded ballroom at her sister Alexandra's annual Children's Fund Ball, she'd known he was destined to be someone very special in her life. They'd danced and drunk champagne, and within hours she'd fallen head over heels in love with a man whose name she didn't even know! No, that wasn't true. She'd fallen in love the moment their eyes had made a connection across the ballroom. And she was fairly sure her lover had felt the same way.

The memory of that perfect evening still made her smile. She'd talked Serena into telling the guards she already had retired to her rooms for the night. And then Elizabeth had led him to the little octagonal pavilion at the far end of the formal gardens.

The glass-walled house was furnished with simple chaise lounges for whiling away long, lazy summer afternoons. One of those lounges would forever linger in her memory. He'd kissed her until she thought she might die of pleasure, and then he'd gently drawn her down onto the chaise and—

"Take me to the princess's table." The brusque, masculine voice penetrated her daydreaming.

"The princess is dining alone, sir. I don't think—"

Her heart began to beat frantically as it recognized her lover's voice. She'd planned on visiting him tomorrow, hadn't expected to see him so soon! She half stood, and her napkin slid to the floor.

But she didn't notice. All her attention was riveted on the man standing in the archway of the dining room.

The man whose steady gaze compelled her not to look away, as memories of their hours together sizzled through the air between them as surely as a silky finger over sensitive skin.

His eyes were a dark, dangerous blue, screened by thick black eyelashes that any woman would have killed for. The last time they'd met, those blue eyes had been warm with desire. Right now, they were flashing with a combination of puzzlement, wariness and what she was pretty sure was a touch of anger.

"Never mind. I see her." His voice was deep and tough as he started forward, completely ignoring the fluttering waiters hovering around him.

"But...sir! You are hardly dressed for—sir! A tie and jacket are required in the dining room...."

As her broad-shouldered lover advanced toward her alcove, she took a deep breath, ignoring the sudden doubts that fluttered through her brain.

He'd be happy to see her. Of course he would. And he'd be as thrilled about the baby as she was.

The baby! Some protective maternal mechanism prompted her to resume her seat. Quickly, she reached for her napkin and draped it over her lap, pulling loose the folds of her tunic so that the barely noticeable swell of her abdomen was hidden. She didn't question the instinct that told her this was not the time to tell him of his impending fatherhood. That could come later. After they'd gotten to know each other better.

The thought made her feel hot all over. Raising her chin, she let the warmth of her feelings show in her eyes as she smiled at the man approaching her table. The man whose set, unsmiling face didn't offer anything remotely resembling the welcome she'd prayed he would extend.

He was huge. That was the first thing that registered now that she'd gotten over the surprise of seeing him so unexpectedly. Oh, she'd remembered he was big, but the man striding toward her, wearing a white T-shirt, faded jeans cinched by a snug leather belt with a heavy silver buckle and dust-covered work boots was simply enormous. But as she focused on his face, she knew he was indeed the man to whom she'd given her heart—and so much more—five months ago.

His hair was raven-black, gleaming in the discreet lighting of the dining room. It had been ruthlessly groomed the night they'd met, but by the time the evening had ended, it had been every bit as rumpled and disheveled as it was right now. Shadows emphasized the hollows beneath high, slanted cheekbones, and his firm lips, lips she remembered curved in a sensual smile, were as full and sensual as ever, though they were pressed into a grim line at the moment.

"How did you find me?"

Whatever she'd expected, that wasn't part of any greeting she could imagine. "Your card," she said, raising her hands helplessly. "The one you left for me."

"I didn't leave you any card."

"Oh, yes, don't you remember? It was on the chaise when I—" She halted in sudden acute embarrassment.

Then the meaning of his denial struck her. *He hadn't meant to leave his card behind. Hadn't intended that she ever know who he was.* The idea was crushing, and for a long moment she couldn't even force herself to form words. Finally, lifting her chin, she put on the most regal expression she possessed, the expression her entire family used to cover emotion from prying eyes and paparazzi. "Apparently I was wrong to assume you intended me to look you up if I was in the States," she said in a cool, smooth voice. "I apologize."

"I told my father years ago I wouldn't marry any of you."

Her face reflected her bewilderment. This conversation was making no sense. "What?" She shook her head. "What are you talking about?"

"About an arranged marriage. To one of the princesses." He crossed his arms and scowled at her. "To *you*." He stabbed a finger in her direction. The move made his muscular arms bulge and the shirt strained at its seams across his chest. He still stood over her, and if he wanted to intimidate her, he was doing a darn good job.

But she wasn't going to let him cow her. Never mind that her hopeful heart was breaking into a thousand little pieces. Thank heavens she hadn't had a chance to share any of her foolish dreams with him. "I didn't come here to marry you," she said in a slow, measured tone that barely squeezed past the lump in her throat.

His expression darkened even more, if that was possible. Slowly, he uncrossed his arms and leaned forward across the table, planting his big palms flat on the surface. He was invading her space and she forced herself not to scoot backwards, away from him.

"I am not amused by your little act," he said through his teeth. "If you came here hoping to take me back to Wynborough like some kind of damned trophy, you can think again, Princess."

It was so far from the passionate greeting that she'd imagined all these months, like a stupid fool, that she had to fight the tears that welled up. What was wrong with him? She hadn't done anything to make him so angry.

"I didn't come here to take you anywhere," she said, swallowing hard to keep the sobs at bay. "I am here on another matter entirely—although I did wish to talk to you."

There was a tense silence. The man who'd been her lover didn't move a muscle for a long second. She felt a tear escape and trickle down her cheek, but she didn't even raise a hand to brush it away. "Who are you, anyway?" she asked in a shaky voice.

He smiled. A wide baring of perfect white teeth that somehow was more of a threat than a pleasantry. Reaching across the table, he picked up her small, fisted hand and bowed low over it. "Raphael Michelangelo Edward Andrew Thorton, Prince of Thortonburg and heir to the Grand Duke of Thortonburg at your service, Your Royal Highness," he said. "As if you didn't know. Expect me for dinner in your suite tomorrow evening at seven."

Before she could pull away, he pressed an overly courteous kiss to the back of her hand, his gaze holding hers. Despite the animosity and antagonism that radiated from his big body, a vivid, detailed image of the intimacy with which those finely chiseled lips had traveled over her body leaped into her head. Her cheeks grew hot and she mentally cursed her fair complexion, because in his eyes flared awareness—he knew exactly what she was thinking.

Then his lips compressed into a thin line as he straightened abruptly. "And be ready to answer my questions this time, *Princess*."

Elizabeth paced the suite nervously as the clock struck seven the following evening. The Prince of Thortonburg! She still couldn't believe it.

As children, she and her sisters had made fun of the stern Grand Duke. She could still remember Serena swaggering across the playroom, doing a deadly accurate imitation of the man, boasting about his eldest son's educational achievements in England and America, that had had Katherine and her in stitches. Even Alexandra, whose overdeveloped sense of responsibility and position as the eldest had often made her seem stuffy to the younger girls, had laughed until the tears ran.

When the girls grew old enough to be presented at court

and began to attend the balls and royal functions of the kingdom, they'd speculated about the invisible Thortonburg heir. Though he wasn't that much older than Alexandra, none of her sisters had ever seen him. He'd been away at Eton and Oxford for years, then to the States to Harvard, she'd heard, and not long after that there had been rumors of a quarrel between the Grand Duke and his elder son. If it weren't for Roland, the personable younger son of the Grand Duke, who vouched for his brother's existence, she would have thought Raphael was a hoax. When he hadn't even shown up for Roland's twenty-first birthday party, it had only fueled the fires of her sisters' curiosity.

Well, he existed, all right. She rested a hand on the slight swell of her belly, hidden beneath the loose, floating gauze of the dress she'd chosen to wear this evening. She could guarantee that he existed.

The worries of the present receded beneath a wave of memories that could still make her blush. She remembered the first time she'd seen him. He'd been wearing severe black evening dress, which had made him look impossibly tall and broad-shouldered compared to every other man in the room, as indeed he was. His only concession to the masquerade ball had been a small black silk mask that concealed the upper half of his face.

She'd been standing across the ballroom, dressed in the costume of a medieval princess, when their eyes had met. Within minutes, he'd cut a decisive path through the crowd to reach her side.

"Good evening, fair lady. Might I have the pleasure of your company in this dance?"

Up close, he was so much larger than she that he could have been intimidating. But as she allowed him to take her gloved hand, his eyes glowed a warm blue through the slits in the mask, and she had felt the oddest sense of security surround her. He drew her into a very correct ballroom position for the waltz that followed, and silently they danced. He didn't even ask her name. Enjoying the game, she preserved the pretense of two strangers, but as the evening progressed, he gently urged her closer to him until she could feel his big hand splayed across her back, his long fingers nearly caressing the upper swell of her bottom, the strength of his muscled thighs pressing against her through the light gown she wore.

They'd danced like that for hours, until every nerve in her body quivered with desire. Her fingers had explored the heavy muscles of his arms and shoulders, slid up into his hair, and she felt his big body shudder against hers.

He brushed a kiss over her ear. "Let's get out of here."

A jolt of need surged through her. Had she ever felt like this before? The answer was so clear—none of the polished suitors who came sniffing around the royal residence had ever made her feel so much as a fraction of what she felt for this man.

She lifted her face to his, studying his thick-lashed eyes through the mask, the clean line of his jaw and the slight curve of chiseled lips. His gaze held hers, demanding her answer, and, as suddenly as that, she knew this was the man with whom she wanted to spend the rest of her life. She'd lifted herself on tiptoe and brazenly brushed her lips over his, then reached back and unlinked his hands from behind her back.

"Just let me visit the powder room," she said. "I'll meet you on the terrace."

But as she turned away, he caught her by the wrist and lifted a big hand to her face, caressing the soft flesh along her cheek with one long finger. "Don't be long," he said in a deep voice that sent shivers of excitement racing through her, and her body contracted in an uncontrollable sexual response.

Turning her head, she kissed his finger as she slipped away. "I won't be," she promised.

And she wasn't. It took her mere moments to locate Serena, flirting cheerfully and shamelessly with a crowd of young men, and she unapologetically drew her aside. "Cover for me tonight. I met someone."

"Who?" Serena's green eyes went wide with anticipation.

But Elizabeth shook her head. "I'll tell you tomorrow. Just cover for me, okay?"

"Okay."

Since they'd been children, the two of them had shared a longing for freedom from the ever-present bodyguards who shadowed their every move. Alexandra, immersed in correctness, and dear, quiet Katherine never seemed to mind the oppressive atmosphere, but she had longed for freedom, as had Serena. It had been a great game to elude the guards, and often, one of them would murmur, "Cover for me," just before committing some daring vanishing act, invariably sending the guards into frantic scurrying which the hidden sister watched with glee.

It wasn't particularly difficult to shake her observers. The royal bodyguards took their work seriously, but they were no match for a young woman who'd had years of practice in evading them.

Slipping out a side door into the garden, she approached the terrace from the lawn, her heart thumping heavily as she recognized her handsome dance partner standing on the other side of the low stone wall of the terrace.

"Hello, there," she murmured.

He turned, immediately picking her out of the darkness and strolling to the edge of the wall. "Hello, beautiful," he said. And in one powerful, lightning-swift move, he vaulted over the wall and dropped to the ground beside her.

She pressed a startled hand to her mouth, then released a nervous laugh. "Some people use the steps," she pointed out, gesturing to the marble stairs at the center of the terrace.

"But you weren't near the stairs," he replied in a perfectly reasonable voice.

She smiled. "No, I wasn't, was I?"

He cupped her elbow, drawing her away from the lights of the terrace and into the dim evening coolness of the gardens. "I thought perhaps you weren't coming."

She caught her breath in dismay, turning to face him and clutching his arm. It suddenly seemed vitally important to reassure him. "I'm sorry. It took longer than I expected. You see, I had to—"

But her words were stilled when he gently placed one large finger against her lips. "Hush. It doesn't matter."

His gaze held hers as he slowly, without any hurry or fumbling, placed his hands at her waist and drew her closer. She found she was holding her breath as his mouth drew nearer and nearer. "I've been wanting to do this all evening," he murmured. His lips were a heartbeat away now, and she found she was holding her breath as she leaned forward the scant distance that separated them and allowed his lips to meet hers.

It was heaven, was all she could think. His mouth was warm and tender, competently molding hers as he gathered her closer. Suddenly, within the space of a second, a flashfire raced through her system as desire spread. She sank against him, and instantly his arms tightened, his mouth grew firmer, less tentative and more demanding. He kissed her as though she were the only thing in his entire world, his tongue invading her mouth in a basic, primitive rhythm that grew stronger, more insistent and demanding until she locked her arms around his shoulders, straining against him as he plundered her lips.

He groaned, deep in his throat, and one hand slid down her back to her bottom, sliding around and over the tender flesh, tracing the crease of her buttocks with one long finger, then clasping her firmly in his hand and lifting her strongly against him. She gasped against his mouth as she felt his hard body pressing into her, the blatant surging against her soft belly and the driving need his shifting hips communicated. She realized her hips were moving, too, slipping back and forth against him as her body sought relief from the need racing through her.

His mouth blazed a trail down her throat, pressing a string of stinging kisses to her collarbone and firmly sliding down over her heated flesh until his face was pressed into the full swell of her breasts. He turned his head, and she jumped as a hot breath seared her tender flesh, and then his mouth began to move again. Her head fell back as he brushed over one straining nipple, suckling her through the thin fabric of her gown, and she moaned, twisting against him, her hands coming up to clutch at his hair, combing restlessly through the black silk strands.

He lifted his head, and he was breathing heavily, harsh gasps for air. "Where can we go?"

His voice was so deep and guttural, it was nearly a growl, and her feminine nature recognized the primitive possession in the sound, her body drawing into a nearly painful knot of need. "The—the garden house," she said breathlessly. "Down this path—oh!"

Before she could complete the sentence, he had lifted her into his arms, his head coming down again, his lips slanting over hers in a complete claim that it never occurred to her to resist. She might not know his name, but her body recognized his. And as he began to stride down the path, she relaxed in his arms and gave herself to the embrace that should have felt strange but only felt…right, as if finally, after twenty-seven years of waiting, she'd found what she hadn't even known she'd been waiting for.

Two

On the dot of seven, Rafe knocked on the door of the Royal Princess of Wynborough's suite. Almost immediately, the double doors swung inward, as if Elizabeth had been waiting on the other side.

Elizabeth. She'd been nameless for five months now. Her real name was going to take some getting used to.

Her eyes widened, and he knew she must be contrasting the image he'd presented yesterday in his work clothes with the charcoal suit he donned now. She shouldn't be that surprised—she'd seen him in a tux.

For that matter, he thought with a surge of grim humor, she'd seen him wearing a whole lot less.

"Good evening," she said, stepping back and waving a hand in invitation for him to enter. "Please come in."

"Thank you, Your Highness." He gave the title the faintest emphasis and was gratified to see a blush climb her neck as he stepped into the room.

She was dressed simply, in a pretty, lightweight dress in

a silky fabric that swirled loosely around her body and draped over the full swells of her breasts, drawing his eye as he passed her. His body sat up and took notice as he remembered the soft mounds that had filled his hands a few months ago.... He mentally shook himself, annoyed that he was letting his sex drive get the better of his good judgment again. Just like the first time he'd seen her.

The Children's Fund Ball was an annual masquerade event, and he still didn't know what had possessed him to attend. Once he'd seen this woman, though, he'd ceased to wonder. He and his mysterious lady had complied with the ball's unspoken rule, not identifying themselves. Still, he was almost positive his paramour had been one of the princesses. Her demeanor had been refined, almost archaically elegant compared to the brash American women whom he'd seen throw themselves at a man. Even compared to other women at the ball, British royals as well as those of his native isle, she'd seemed exceptionally genteel.

If she were one of the princesses, that would make sense. He'd never even met one of them, despite his own royal status. Granted, they were all several years younger than he, and he'd been away at school most of his life before he'd escaped Thortonburg, but rumor had it that King Phillip employed the tightest security to keep his remaining family safe.

Rafe supposed that if *his* infant son had been kidnapped and presumably killed, he'd be overprotective with his other children, too. Yes, given all those factors, he'd been nearly positive that his lady fair had been one of King Phillip's four beautiful daughters.

"Could I offer you a drink?" She had moved across the room behind him and now stood behind the small breakfast bar.

"Please." He walked to the bar and hooked one foot around a stool, drawing it to him and propping himself on the edge of the seat with his feet splayed. "Nice place."

"Yes. It's very comfortable."

"I guess you wouldn't know what it's like to live somewhere that wasn't."

Her eyes flickered to his for an instant. "I've never had the opportunity to find out," she said in a neutral tone. Busying herself for a moment, she laid a napkin on the bar and set a highball glass in front of him.

He stared at the drink for a minute. "How do you know what I drink?"

The color that had begun to subside began to climb her neck again. "If you'd prefer another drink, that's fine. This is what you were drinking...the last time."

"This is fine." Abruptly, he picked up the drink and took a quick gulp. When she'd first seen him yesterday in the restaurant, there had been warm, intimate welcome in the depths of her green eyes until he'd scared it away. Today, the same wide eyes held only wariness. Her hair was a beautiful copper, shiny as a new American penny. Tonight she wore it down, curling softly around her shoulders and framing her heart-shaped face.

He recognized that face. Now that he knew who she was, he felt like an idiot for doubting his instincts before. It could almost have been her mother's face at a younger age, except for a slight dimple in her chin, courtesy of her father, the king.

The king.

Anger began to rise again and he ruthlessly pushed it back and shut the door on it. He intended to have his questions answered this evening.

Elizabeth continued to hover behind the bar. She had made herself a drink as well, though he'd seen her put nothing in it but cranberry juice. She gestured to the center of the room, where a coffee table surrounded by several chairs and love seats held a silver tray full of canapés. "Shall we sit down?"

He rose from the stool and gestured for her to precede him. "Certainly."

Her gaze flew to his, then whisked away again, and he saw her swallow. Then she stepped from behind the bar and quickly walked to one of the chairs, sinking down and demurely crossing her legs at the ankle while she fussed with the loose folds of her oversize dress.

Rafe followed her, taking a seat at an angle to hers and accepting the plate she offered him. He'd worked all day and had only gotten home in time to shower and change before heading over to the hotel, and he was starving. As he filled his plate with a selection of the hors d'ouevres, he glanced at her. "Aren't you going to eat?"

She gave a single nervous shake of her head. "I'm not particularly hungry. You go ahead."

"If you're sure." This rigid courtesy was getting to him already. One more of the reasons he didn't intend to return to Thortonburg.

She only nodded.

There was an uncomfortable silence for a few moments. Judging from the way she fidgeted, it bothered her a lot more than it did him. He applied himself to his food until his plate was empty, but he held up a hand in refusal when she offered him a second helping.

"No thanks, this will hold me for the moment."

A faint smile crossed her face. "As you wish." She studied him curiously. "You're very American, aren't you?"

He supposed she meant the slang expression, because he knew his voice still carried the clipped accents of his homeland. "This is my home now," was all he said.

"This country appeals to you so much more than Thortonburg?" she asked softly.

"When I was younger, anyplace that didn't have my father in it was appealing," he said with grim self-mockery. "Now...yes, I like it here. It's warm, it's sunny almost all the time—you certainly can't say that for the North Atlantic.'' Only a short distance off the coast of the United Kingdom, the country of his birth was frequently rainy, cloudy and chilly. On its good days.

"No." Again, a small smile played around her lips. "You certainly can't."

He watched her lips curve, aware of the flare of sexual attraction deep in his gut. She was every bit as beautiful as he remembered, and every bit as seductive. His good humor faded.

"Why did you seduce me?" he asked bluntly.

Her green eyes widened and her head snapped up as if he'd struck her. Her face went white, then vivid color filled every centimeter of her fair complexion. "I didn't seduce you!"

He considered that. "Okay. I'll give you that. It was definitely a two-sided deal, as I recall."

For a moment, she simply stared at him silently and he watched, fascinated, as a deep rosy hue flushed her cheeks. Finally, in the same neutral voice she'd used a minute ago, she said, "Why ever would I want to seduce you?"

"Does the word *betrothal* ring any bells?"

She had a bewildered look on her face as she shook her head. "But I'm not betrothed to anyone."

He snorted. "Do we have to continue this little game of make-believe? Okay, so it didn't have to be *you*. My father isn't particular as long as the union occurs. You know full well one of you will marry the future Grand Duke one day. You were trying to get a jump on your sisters, weren't you? After all, if you can't have a king, a grand duke is the next best thing."

"You think I'd marry for a *title?*" She gaped at him for a moment, ignoring the rest of his heavy-handed sarcasm. "My father never arranged a marriage in his life. I don't know why you believe he would do something like that."

"Maybe because my father's been telling me since I was

four years old that I would marry one of the princesses one day?''

''We'll marry whomever we want, your father's wishes aside.''

''Umm-hmm.'' It was a skeptical sound.

''There was no arrangement of any kind!'' she insisted. ''Anyway, my eldest sister is already married. She married a rancher from right here in Arizona. They're expecting their first child—''

''I don't give a bloody damn if they're expecting ten children,'' he said through his teeth.

Her eyes widened again and though she didn't actually move, he had the impression she'd reared back out of his reach.

''You're...what? Second eldest?'' he asked.

She nodded. ''Third, actually. My brother was—*is*—the eldest. Katherine and Serena are younger than I am.''

Why had Elizabeth been steered his way instead of one of her sisters? It was a puzzle that he couldn't find the right pieces for, and he didn't like unfinished puzzles. But for now, he set it aside. ''My father and your father must have gotten their heads together since I left the country,'' he said. ''And you were the sacrificial lamb. I wonder how the King decided which daughter to send. A roll of dice? A flipped coin?''

''I told you my father would never arrange a marriage for me,'' she insisted, and her voice was agitated. ''There is no scheme.''

''Not anymore there isn't,'' he said, not caring how cold and implacable he sounded. ''You might have been a virgin, and you might even have been the hottest sex I've ever had, but I'm still not falling for it. Go home and tell your daddy I'm not marrying you.''

The color that had infused her cheeks drained away. For a minute, he thought she was going to cry. Then she drew a deep breath. ''I'll tell my father nothing of the sort.'' She leaped to her feet and stomped across the room, yanking open the door of the suite. "He didn't plot for us to meet *or* marry, and if you think I'm trying to trap you into matrimony you couldn't be more wrong. You may leave, sir, and don't come back. I plan to forget we ever met." Grandly, she flung her arm wide to encourage him to leave.

About to take her up on the invitation, Rafe rose from the chair—and stopped in his tracks, all thoughts of leaving forgotten. His eyes narrowed in disbelief.

She was pregnant.

Shock ripped through him as the silhouette of the princess was outlined through her thin dress against the light flowing in from the hall...the light that clearly showed the bulge of pregnancy beneath the flowing style he'd assumed was merely fashionable. Her outflung arm pulled the garment tight across her midsection, making it impossible to miss her condition.

Temporarily struck dumb, Rafe stalked across the room toward her.

Elizabeth must have recognized the bone-deep rage tearing through him, because she backed up until the wall beside the door stopped her retreat.

He didn't hesitate until he was practically standing on her toes, the protrusion of her belly only inches from his body and her wide, fear-filled eyes gazing up at him defensively.

"You...little...*bitch,*" he ground out. "So *that's* what this surprise reunion is all about. You've got a bun in the oven and let me guess..." He paused and allowed a mocking grin to slide across his face. "I'm supposed to believe it's mine."

She gasped. When her hands came up and shoved hard at his stomach, he was surprised enough that he let her push him back a step or two. Again, she was flushing that bright red that only a redhead could manage, her whole body shaking. Her face looked shattered, and he thought she was going to cry, but when she spoke, her voice trembled with rage. "It *is* your child," she said. "My sister Serena thought it was only fair that you know."

Her words rocked him to the core, but he managed to cover his reaction with a sneer. "And you expect me to believe that? Do I really look like that big a sucker?" He crossed his arms and his own rising anger made his voice rough. "That could be anybody's baby."

Her eyes darkened, dulled, and she swayed. Alarmed, he reached out to steady her, but she backed away from him so quickly that she nearly fell over a chair. She slapped his hand away.

"As you so kindly reminded me, I was a virgin." Her voice was low and unsteady, and her body shook from head to toe. He had a moment's instinctive concern for her condition, but before he could think of anything to say that might calm her a little, she whipped around and ran across the suite to a far door, entering it and slamming the door so hard the frame shook.

Considering she'd caught him by surprise, he reacted quickly, sprinting after her. But she'd had just enough of a start that by the time he reached for the doorknob, he heard the distinct metallic click of a lock and then the final hammering sound of a deadbolt being thrown into place.

"Elizabeth!" he roared, rattling the knob. "Come out here!"

There was no answer, but through the door he could hear the sound of water running in the bathroom. And then another sound. Weeping. He rested his fists against the door, fighting the urge to batter it down. Frustration and fury mounted as the feeling of being trapped rose within him. Any sympathy that her crying had aroused died as echoes of his childhood swamped him. He'd sworn he would never have a child, would never do to a child what had been done to him. *Never.*

He gave the door a hefty kick with the flat of his foot.

"Nobody makes my life plans for me!" he shouted through the door before he spun on his heel. "Not my father, and not you!"

His mood was only marginally better at nine the next morning. He had tossed and turned half the bloody night. This morning, his eyes felt gritty and he was drinking industrial-strength coffee in an effort to revive the brain cells that were comatose from lack of sleep.

But there were a few brain cells that were alive and well. With no effort at all, he could recall the look on Elizabeth's face when he'd told her that the baby she carried could belong to anyone.

She'd been shattered.

He felt like pond scum. He might not have any intention of marrying the girl, but he wasn't a total jerk. He knew, as sure as he knew his own name, that she'd never had another lover. Before him, impossible. After him... If she'd been a bedhopper, she wouldn't still have been a virgin when he had met her. He wasn't sure how old she was, but he knew she had to be in her mid-twenties. Definitely not promiscuous.

And her baby was his.

My sister Serena thought it was only fair that you know. What in bloody hell did that mean? That Elizabeth wouldn't have told him otherwise?

He might not want it, might be furious about this whole bloody mess, but he wasn't a man who walked away from his responsibilities. He'd fathered a child, and he'd support it. She'd waited, damn her, far too long for abortion to be an option. He'd counted in his head during the endless nighttime hours, and he figured she was about five months along now.

Abortion. In his heart, he knew he couldn't let her do that, anyway. It certainly would have been the easy way out, but the solution gave him a sick feeling. Together, he and Elizabeth Wyndham had created a life, and he didn't believe either of them had the right to end it.

No. Biologically, he was going to be a father, though he had no intention of getting involved in this child's life. He wondered if Elizabeth had considered adoption. As far as he was concerned, that would be the best thing all around, but somehow, he doubted his redheaded lover would see it that way. Nor would the royal family, come to think of it.

Oh, well. If she wanted to raise the kid, he couldn't stop her. And he certainly wouldn't have any trouble supporting it financially. Even though he'd refused to use any of his family's money, except that from his grandmother's trust, he'd managed to build quite a respectable business for himself here in the States. Regardless of the hidebound, ambitious schemer he had the misfortune to call his father.

Hell. He wasn't going to get any more sleep, and he knew he couldn't work until he'd straightened things out with Elizabeth. Dumping the coffee in the sink, he grabbed his car keys and headed for the garage.

Twenty-five minutes later, he stood in the suite where he'd been only last night, clinging to his temper by a thin thread while the personal assistant provided to Elizabeth during her hotel stay spread her hands helplessly. "I'm sorry, Mr. Thorton, but the princess insisted. I didn't think it was wise for her to rent a car for herself, but there was simply no stopping her."

"How many were in her party?"

"Her party? Oh, no one else, sir. She was alone."

She hadn't even taken a driver or a bodyguard? The vague tingle of apprehension that had hovered since he'd learned the princess had left the hotel that morning became a full-fledged itch. "What about her bodyguard?"

"She didn't bring one, sir."

Rafe swore, a string of curses that clearly shocked the young woman before him. "Where did she go?"

"I don't know, sir. She was meeting a man, I believe.

All she told me was that she planned to be back by the dinner hour.''

Dinner hour. In Wynborough, that could easily mean eight or nine in the evening. No way was he waiting that long to be sure she was all right. With the hotel employee to vouch for him, it was an easy task to get the concierge to supply him with Elizabeth's intended destination and to get a description of the vehicle she was driving.

Driving! As sheltered as her life had been, he would bet she'd rarely, if ever, driven herself anywhere in her whole life.

Not to mention the little fact that Americans drove on the other side of the road from what she was accustomed at home.

As he waited impatiently for the facts he'd requested, the assistant's other words sank in. Meeting a man. A man! Who the hell would Elizabeth know in Phoenix other than him? She was pregnant with *his* baby, damn it!

Five minutes later, he was climbing back into his truck and heading for the highway.

He drove south out of Phoenix on Interstate 10, heading toward Casa Grande. The concierge had told him that Elizabeth had asked for directions to Catalina, a little town nestled between the Tortolita mountain range and the Coronado National Forest just north of Tucson. She had maybe an hour's start on him—how the hell was he going to find her?

Especially if she was meeting some other man.

It was only with the greatest restraint that he could keep himself from snarling at the woman's naïveté. She didn't know the first thing about men. Elizabeth had no business haring off to meet another man, and when he found her he was going to let her know in no uncertain terms that as the father of her baby, he wouldn't tolerate another man hanging around his...

His what?

Nothing, he told himself. *Nothing.* She doesn't belong to you. You need this princess in your life like you need heat rash.

It was hot.

She didn't think she'd ever experienced this kind of heat before. She'd vacationed on islands in warm climates, but nothing she could recall resembled this dry, draining heat that leached every ounce of energy from her. Of course, she'd never been on a tropical island when she was pregnant, either, and she'd nearly always had a pool or a beautiful ocean in which to cool off.

Elizabeth bent over the motor of the rental car again. This was dreadful. She had no idea what she might be looking for among all the black, greasy parts and metal pipes. All she knew was that a white, billowing cloud of smoke had begun to leak from beneath the bonnet of the automobile about thirty minutes ago, and that when she'd pulled off the road to investigate the sedan wouldn't start again.

Fear coiled and her fingers shook as she tentatively reached forward and lightly tapped a piece of metal. It was easy to call herself a dunce. An hour ago, a jaunt down an American highway to find the man who might be her brother had sounded like a grand lark. Now it sounded like the height of folly.

No chauffeur. No bodyguard. No car phone. Off the main road on a little side highway with not a building in sight. Her parents would be terribly distressed if they knew. It hadn't seemed so foolish to her when she'd had the idea. She was so awfully weary of being followed, escorted, fussed over everywhere she went. This had seemed like the perfect time to see how it felt to be *normal.*

Now all she could think was that if someone would rescue her, she'd offer him a title in his own right. Peering into the engine one more time, she picked up the black umbrella she'd brought along and held it open above her head, providing a bit of shade from the sun if not from the heat.

The thought of what Rafe would say if he were here only served to lower her spirits even more. He thought she was a silly, helpless girl who'd been sheltered from the real world her entire life. She could see his disdain in his eyes when he looked at her.

Was he right? She thought of the organ donor campaign with which she'd consented to work, of the hospital visits she'd made in the name of her other charity, a hospice in Wynborough's capital city. She'd seen suffering. She'd seen death. She wasn't a hothouse flower who had fluff for brains.

Oh? Then why are you standing here in the heat beside a crippled auto?

She was going to pray to God Rafe never found out about this. Then again, why should he? When he'd slammed out of her suite last night, she'd known she would never see him again.

Far down the road, something distracted her from her morose thoughts. A car! A car on the highway coming toward her. It was moving quite fast over the straight, flat terrain, and as it drew closer she could see it was a truck. Not that it mattered as long as the driver would be willing to take her to Catalina. In Catalina she could accomplish her goal, which was to locate Samuel Flynn, the man who once was an orphan in The Sunshine Home for Children, the home she and her sisters were sure their kidnapped brother had been brought thirty years ago.

Her stomach quivered, and she hoped it was at the thought of locating her brother, presumed dead for so long. What a coronation anniversary gift that would make for her father!

Her stomach quivered again, and she wiped a drop of sweat from her temple before it could trickle down her cheek. The truck was drawing to a halt behind her car now, and she squinted as the driver stepped out, forcing her dry lips into a welcoming smile. Until she recognized the big broad-shouldered figure of the Prince of Thortonburg walking toward her.

Curses. The day was rapidly assuming the proportions of a major disaster. She closed her eyes, hoping he was a mirage, but she was forced to open them quickly by a wave of vertigo. He was still there.

His expression was forbidding as he strode toward her. "What do you think you're doing?" he demanded.

"It's lovely to see you again, too, Mr. Thorton. How coincidental that you should be traveling the same road as I." She tilted her chin, determined not to give him the satisfaction of seeing her squirm.

"You know perfectly well it's not coincidence. I was coming after you. You have no business traipsing around an American desert without an escort."

"Thank you for your opinion. Where I traipse and with whom is not your concern, sir." She would have stuck her nose even higher in the air, but she was forced to close her eyes as another round of dizziness seized her.

"Elizabeth!" She felt his big hands catch her elbows.

"You may address me as 'Your Royal Highness'—oh!" She squeaked in alarm as Rafe scooped her up in his arms and swung her around, and she clutched at his shoulders as the world spun crazily around her. "Put me down!"

"Gladly." His booted feet crunched on gravel as he set her on her feet, and she opened a cautious eye to see that he had brought her around to the passenger side of his truck. Keeping one arm about her, he leaned around her and opened the door, then set his hands at her waist and easily lifted her into the enclosed cab.

He'd left the engine and the air conditioner running. Beneath her legs in her thin dress the leather seat was cool, and she was blessedly shaded from the vicious sun. She almost whimpered with delight, but she wasn't going to give him the satisfaction. Instead, she lay her head against the back of her seat and blotted her forehead with a tissue from her purse.

"What's wrong with the car?" he asked.

"I don't know," she said. "I was trying to figure that out when you came along."

"Right." He gave a snort of amusement. "Why did you stop along the road in the middle of nowhere?"

"There was smoke coming from beneath the bonnet."

"Smoke?" He looked alarmed. "Are you sure it wasn't steam?"

She shrugged. "I haven't a clue. Smoke, steam, something like that."

"There's a pretty big difference," he informed her. Then he straightened. "Put your seat belt on." He slammed the passenger door with more force than necessary, making her wince.

She watched through the windshield as he walked back to the blue Lincoln and retrieved the keys before locking its door and coming back to the big truck. Today he was wearing jeans again, jeans that caressed the solidly muscled contours of his legs like a lover's hands. She remembered the feel of those strong limbs against hers, the heat of his skin and the rough texture of the hair liberally sprinkled over it. The feminine core of her tightened with pleasure, but she sternly reminded herself that theirs had been a single encounter, that the Prince of Thortonburg had made it abundantly clear that she was going to be no part of his life.

A lump in her throat warned her to change the direction of her thoughts, and as Rafe approached the truck, she catalogued the rest of his clothing. With the jeans, he had donned a white shirt, the sleeves of which he'd turned back several times. On his head was a broad-brimmed white straw hat like American cowboys wore. And, as he had since she'd first seen him again, he was wearing a pair of boots. She'd noticed last night that even with his suit he'd worn a polished pair of black leather boots with intricate stitching.

He slid easily into the driver's seat and fastened his own seat belt before backing the truck up and turning a wide circle in the highway.

"Wait! I want to go to Catalina," she said.

"Tough." He didn't even look at her. "You're coming back to Phoenix and going to the doctor, then you're going to lie down and rest."

"To the doctor?" She gaped at him. "I don't need a doctor."

"I want you to be looked over anyway," he said. "You were mighty close to heatstroke back there." He reached behind the seat and pulled a thermos forward. "Drink. You didn't even have extra water with you," he said in a scathing tone.

"I'm not used to the climate here," she said with quiet dignity. "I'm aware that you think I'm a brainless fool, so you can stop rubbing my nose in it."

"Princess," he said, "I haven't even started. What in hell are you thinking, running around here without a bodyguard?"

"I don't need a bodyguard," she said through clenched teeth. "I'm perfectly capable of taking care of myself. And anyway the hotel assistant and the concierge knew my destination."

"They wouldn't have been much help if you'd spent hours out here in the sun."

The only answer to that was silence, and she turned her head to gaze out the window, closing her eyes to shut him out.

She must have napped, because she woke, groggy and disoriented, as they were entering the outskirts of Phoenix.

Hastily, she straightened in her seat, hoping he hadn't noticed.

"Have a good nap?"

So much for wishes. She didn't answer him.

"Why were you going to Catalina?"

She was growing mightily sick of his constant interrogations. "I wanted to visit the next of my many lovers to see if he could be the father of my child," she snapped.

There was a moment of silence in the truck, a silence that nearly vibrated with electricity.

"I apologize," he said in a low growl. "I know it's my child."

He did? Momentarily stunned, she turned her head to stare at him. He glanced over at her and his blue eyes were dark and sober. He looked nearly as shocked as she felt.

There didn't seem to be much to say after that. She went back to staring out the window, though she was no longer seeing the landscape that was so foreign to her, no longer enjoying the contrast between what she'd grown up with and the stark, dry, blindingly bright Arizona desert.

He believed her. That one thought kept running through her mind, and she wondered what had convinced him. Yesterday he'd appeared to doubt her claim. The memory of her naïveté made her wince inwardly, and she took a deep breath to stave off the tears that wanted to rise again.

She'd promised herself last night that Rafe Thorton, under whatever name he chose to use, was never going to make her cry again. She'd been stupid and she'd learned a lesson from her stupidity. Several, in fact.

"How do you feel?" Rafe's voice broke into her thoughts, gruff and deep and distinctly noncommittal.

As if you care, she thought.

"Fine, thank you." She made her voice as chilly as possible while still being scrupulously polite.

"You're not used to this climate," he stated. "You'll

have to be doubly careful of the heat, especially in your condition.''

"Thank you for the advice. I'm sure it will prove invaluable.''

His mouth tightened and she was pleased to see that she was annoying him. He didn't speak to her again, but picked up the phone that was installed in the truck and punched in a number, then tapped his fingers impatiently against the wheel while he waited.

She wondered who he was calling, then decided she didn't really care. But she couldn't prevent herself from glancing over at him.

"Hey, gorgeous!" Rafe suddenly became animated. Apparently someone had answered on the other end. Someone female, she suspected, from the way his face relaxed and his teeth flashed in a grin that sent an arrow through her heart. He'd smiled at *her* like that once, she remembered.

And you fell for it, dummy.

"In the desert," he said and she reasoned that the woman had asked him where he was. "Listen," he said, "I have a weird question. I need to know the name and number of a reputable obstetrician in Phoenix."

There was silence on his end and one black eyebrow quirked up, then he laughed, a low and intimate chuckle that set Elizabeth's teeth on edge. "A friend," he said. "That's all you need to know."

He scrabbled in the side pocket on his door and came up with a piece of paper and a pencil, tossing them at Elizabeth. "Write this down," he mouthed.

She glared at him, but as he repeated the name and number she did take them down, then slid the paper back across the seat to him.

"Okay, babe. You're one in a million. I'll call you later today." Removing the phone from his ear, he punched the button to cut off the connection and let it dangle from his fingers for a moment while he drove. Then he studied the information on the paper and dialed again.

While he was talking, Elizabeth sat in miserable silence. Could things get any worse? Obviously, Rafe had a girl-friend, or someone special in his life. The silly fantasies she'd woven about him—about them together—seemed pathetic and ridiculous now. How could she have been so stupid? She might have led a somewhat sheltered life, but she knew what the world was like. Men got women pregnant every day of the week because they acted on sexual attraction without thinking. The resulting condition had nothing to do with affection or love or respect or long-term plans.

Now she was another one of those sad statistics, and her child would be fatherless because of her carelessness.

The words *appointment this morning,* penetrated her absorption, and she was startled into looking over at Rafe again.

"No! I don't need a doctor."

He ignored her.

"I won't go." She tugged at his forearm to get his attention. A mistake. Beneath her fingers, his bare flesh was hot, and the thick hair that grew along his arm was silky in texture.

"Cancel it," she said fiercely.

"Thorton," he said to the person on the phone. "Elizabeth Thorton."

Her fingers clenched on his arm. Then she realized she was still holding on to him and she snatched back her hand. Again his eyebrow slid up into a bold dark arch as he threw her a questioning look. But before she could find her voice, he'd concluded the call and hung up again.

"What are you doing?" she demanded.

"Making you a doctor's appointment," he said easily. "I want to make sure you and the baby are none the worse for wear after spending the morning standing in the sun."

"I don't need a doctor. Go on back to your girlfriend and leave me alone." She tried to infuse the words with command, but even to her she sounded weak and cranky.

"My girlfriend..." He shot her a smug grin. "That was my secretary on the phone. She has twin grandsons, so she's not exactly competition."

"I'm not competing." So there. "Why didn't you use my real name?"

"Would you rather I'd given your real name?" he asked.

She drew in a sharp breath as his words penetrated, then slumped back against the seat. "No," she admitted in a muted tone. "My parents don't know yet."

"Mind if I ask how long you were going to wait?" He sounded more than slightly shocked.

"I wanted to tell you first," she said quietly. "When I get home, there won't be any reason to delay."

"You're going home soon?"

Did she imagine the slight sharpness in his tone? She shrugged. "As soon as my business here is concluded."

"Your business in Catalina? You never did tell me why you were going there."

"No," she said with more calm than she felt. "I didn't."

Three

She wasn't one bit happy with him, Rafe reflected as he unlocked the door of his Phoenix home shortly after lunch. He eyed the rigid line of Elizabeth's back and the regal tilt of her small, dimpled chin. They didn't call her Princess for nothing.

When she'd realized that despite her protests he was adamant about taking her to a doctor, she'd become quietly furious. Through the appointment, and the quick lunch they'd had afterward, she hadn't spoken one word to him beyond the absolute minimum civility required. If she appreciated his concern for protecting her anonymity, it sure didn't show.

Now he ushered her into his spacious foyer, wondering what she thought of the skylights that let in the bright, cheerful sunlight, the flagstone floors and the soft pastel colors of the desert that he'd wanted for his private spaces. He'd designed it himself, initially intending to use it as a display for potential clients. But he'd liked it so much, he hadn't been able to part with it in the end.

Elizabeth halted about three feet into the foyer and turned to face him. "May I use your telephone, please? I'll put any charges on my calling card."

He glared at her, oddly disappointed that she didn't even seem to notice his home, and irritated that she would bring up a silly thing like telephone charges. "The phone is right through here."

He showed her into his casually appointed den, then left her to go into the kitchen and get each of them a cold drink. The doctor had felt that Elizabeth was in good condition although he had advised her to drink plenty of fluids while she was in Arizona, a dictate Rafe fully intended to see she followed.

From his vantage point around the corner he could clearly hear Elizabeth's conversation. His upbringing and conscience protested the eavesdropping, but since she wouldn't talk to him, he told himself he'd have to find out all he could through any method available.

"Yes, this is Elizabeth. Is my mother there?"

A ten-pound load dropped from Rafe's shoulders. So she wasn't calling another man! She was calling her parents. Not that it mattered terribly to him, he assured himself.

"Mummy? Hello, it's Eliz—yes, yes, I'm fine. Yes, I was afraid you'd worry since I didn't call on time. Oh, please don't cry. Mummy? Maybe you'd better put Daddy on the line."

There was a pause, and Rafe remembered to clink a few ice cubes around in the glasses so she wouldn't think he was spying.

"Hello, Daddy. Of course I'm fine. I'm sorry I didn't call first thing this morning as I promised. I rented a car but it broke down on a highway while I was on a little day trip. But I'm fine. I've met someone you know. Well, I suppose he's an American now, but he was from Thorton-burg once. He calls himself Rafe Thorton now, but you know him as the Prince of Thortonburg. What's that? Oh, no, I doubt I'll see much of him. It was really more of a courtesy call on his part—Rafe!'' She glared at him as he removed the receiver from her hand and held it to his own ear.

''Hello, Your Majesty. This is Thorton.'' He knew he sounded clipped and discourteous, but talking to King Phillip was the last thing he'd planned on doing today. Or any day, for that matter.

''Hello, Raphael.'' The King's voice sounded warm and cordial. ''It's been far too long. The States must agree with you.'' He didn't sound annoyed, particularly.

''Give me that!'' Elizabeth reached for the phone he'd taken out of her hand, but he held it above her head until she hissed at him and backed off.

He couldn't resist grinning at her as he returned the receiver to his ear. She might pretend to be a lady, but there was fire beneath her calm surface. ''Excuse me, Your Majesty. I rescued your daughter this morning from a spot of folly. Did she tell you she had no bodyguard or driver with her?''

''No one at all?'' King Phillip sounded alarmed, but not particularly surprised. ''I'm afraid Elizabeth doesn't fully understand how careful she must be. She and her youngest sister spent hours trying to outwit their bodyguards as children. She'd become quite adept at sneaking about, and it's made her a bit overconfident.''

''I agree, Your Majesty. I was a bit concerned myself.''

''Thank you for your assistance.'' The monarch's tones were as friendly as Rafe remembered from his childhood. He never had been able to understand how a man who appeared as nice as the King could conspire with a man as class-conscious as his own father. ''Elizabeth will soon be leaving. I believe the dedication ceremony occurred yesterday.''

"It did." Rafe hesitated. He should be leaping at the chance to get the princess out of his hair, but the thought of her flying back to Wynborough, thousands of miles away, bothered him. He needed more time to think, to decide how to handle this sticky situation with her and the baby before he let her get away.

"Sir, I don't believe the princess should fly right now," he said, turning his broad back on Elizabeth's accusatory face. "She was through a bit of an ordeal this morning. Nothing serious, of course, but I'd be happy to offer her my hospitality until she feels herself again."

"Thank you, Raphael." The King sounded relieved. "That's quite kind of you to look after her for us."

"It will be my pleasure to look after her," he said, turning to pin Elizabeth with a meaningful glance.

Her fair skin colored. She avoided his gaze as she reached for the phone, which he let her have this time. "Daddy, I'm twenty-seven years old," she said into the receiver. "I hardly think I need looking after. In fact, I'd planned on leaving Phoenix today. I want to do a little sightseeing and then I'll be returning to Mitch and Alexandra's for a few days before I come home." She laughed a little, but to Rafe's ears it was a forced sound. "Yes, I know I'm the only one left. No, I promise I won't run off with a cowboy."

Damn right she wouldn't, he thought.

After a few more exchanges, she punched the button that ended the call and replaced the phone in its cradle. For a moment she simply stood, one hand on the receiver, and Rafe could practically feel the weariness radiating from her.

"Have you a telephone book?" she asked without looking at him.

"What for?''

She sighed. "Not that it's any of your business, but I'd like to call a taxi and return to the hotel."

"No."

Clearly startled, she turned and stared at him. "Excuse me?"

"I don't think you should return to the hotel right now." His brain was racing a mile a minute. "You look exhausted. Why don't I show you to a guest room and you can rest for a little while, then I'll take you back when you're refreshed."

She hesitated. "No, I really—"

"I insist," he broke in smoothly. Without giving her a chance to argue further, he took her elbow and led her down the wide wood-floored hall to the second room on the left. "Consider this yours for the time being," he said.

Elizabeth looked around, then turned to survey him suspiciously. "Why do I get the feeling you're plotting something?"

"You have an overactive imagination," he said, shrugging.

She stared at him for a second longer, then let out her breath in a long sigh. "Thank you for your offer. I'll just rest for a little while, and then I can get myself back to the hotel."

He shut her in the bedroom before she could change her mind, hoping she didn't notice that he hadn't agreed. Then he strolled back to the kitchen and picked up the telephone. She wasn't going anywhere.

When she woke, it was twilight. Twilight! Momentarily panicked, not recognizing the quietly attractive room around her, she sprang out of the bed—

And had to sit back down quickly when the room spun around her.

As she sat waiting for the alarming vertigo to abate,

memory sneaked back. A second glance around the room confirmed her recall. This wasn't a hotel room. She was in a guest bedroom at Rafe Thorton's home.

She glanced at her watch and was appalled to see it was after six. She'd slept the entire afternoon away!

There was a telephone on the table beside the bed and she decided she'd better use it while she had the chance. Fishing the paper with Sam Flynn's number on it out of her bag, she quickly punched the buttons.

It was an office number, she realized when an answering machine picked up. And as she listened to the message, her heart sank. Mr. Flynn would be out of town on business for several days. Emergency calls were referred to another number.

Somehow, she didn't think another person could help her. She'd just have to wait until Sam was back again.

A spacious bath off the bedroom afforded her the opportunity to freshen up before she twisted the doorknob and stepped into the hall. She had to resist the urge to tiptoe as she walked into the comfortably decorated family room.

Rafe was nowhere in sight. A pass-through counter at one side of the room connected it with the kitchen so she walked through the nearby doorway. She had to admit, his taste was impeccable. Done in a blond wood that complemented the muted tones echoed in the family room, Rafe's kitchen was sleek and modern yet still warm and inviting.

Wide French doors at one end led to a covered terrace, beyond which lay a glistening blue pool. And in the pool, she could see a dark head and powerful arms that were rhythmically slicing through the water. Rafe.

The muscles in her stomach contracted involuntarily, and her breasts felt as if they tightened as well, drawing her flesh taut and smooth as if waiting to welcome him.

No! How dumb could one woman be? How pathetic? He'd made it more than plain that he didn't want her. Stupid as it had been, she'd come here hoping, maybe even expecting him to greet her with…affection. Warmth. She'd dreamed of his delight at learning she carried his child and of how he'd cuddle and coddle her through the rest of the pregnancy.

Well, she wasn't dreaming anymore. And the ache that seemed to have settled permanently around her heart was only because her child was going to grow up without the traditional family she'd believed was possible.

Opening one of the doors, she stepped through onto the terrace.

Immediately Rafe altered his pattern, cutting through the pool to the side nearest her. "Welcome back," he said, a grin lighting his chiseled features and giving him the handsome, roguish look she remembered so well. "I thought maybe you'd sleep straight through 'til tomorrow."

"Hardly." She kept her voice low and expressionless. "I wanted to thank you for your hospitality. I'll be leaving as soon as I can get a cab out here."

"Elizabeth…" He said her name in a hesitant manner at odds with his usual imperiousness.

"Yes?"

"You're going to have a hard time getting a cab out here."

"Not if I make the deal sweet enough." She spoke with the confidence born of growing up with money and seeing its tiresomely predictable effect on people.

"The thing is…" He let his voice trail off as he put both hands on the side of the pool and smoothly lifted himself from the water, the powerful muscles in his back and shoulders flexing and bulging and sliding over each other in a way that made her mouth go dry and her heart thump in her breast.

He straightened, taking the single step that brought him to her side. His wet bathing trunks molded steely thighs, defining well-remembered muscle. Little drops of water caught in his eyelashes, his beard stubble, clung to his wide shoulders. The water caught in the curls springing from his chest succumbed to gravity's pull and began a steady trickle downward to his navel and below.

She had to force herself not to let her gaze follow the droplets' path. Instead, she repeated, "The thing is...?"

"The thing is," he said again, "you don't have a room to return to anymore."

"I don't—*what?* What do you mean?"

Rafe crossed his arms. Part of her instinctively recognized the defensive posture and her own body tensed in response.

"I checked you out of the hotel," he said.

Surely he couldn't have said what she thought he'd said. She stared at him. "I beg your pardon?"

"Your bags are in the front hallway."

"Are you crazy?" She spun around and stalked back into the house, needing visual confirmation of his claim. Sure enough, the two big bags and smaller grip she'd brought from Alexandra's were sitting in his foyer.

Furious, she stalked back to where he dripped water on the kitchen floor. "What do you think you're doing?" By the slimmest of margins she caught hold of her temper and reined it in.

"Keeping you here for a while," he said bluntly.

"Keeping me...for what purpose?"

"Because," he said, and though his tone sounded reasonable and courteous, she got the impression he was gritting his teeth. "You can't waltz into my life again, announce that you're carrying my child and just leave."

"I made no such announcement," she muttered.

"What did you say?" He took her by the arms and turned her to face him, and she was overwhelmed by the power of his physical presence.

"You can't keep me here against my will." She tried to ignore the tanned flesh of the naked chest only inches in front of her. Turning to the side, she twisted in an attempt to slide from his grip. But Rafe didn't let go. Instead, he pulled her the few inches remaining between their bodies until she was held firmly against him.

Elizabeth gasped as the water droplets clinging to his body and the soaking fabric of his swim trunks quickly penetrated her thin clothing. She closed her eyes, hoping he hadn't seen in her eyes the way this sham of an embrace affected her senses.

Leaning away from him, she attempted to step back, but Rafe didn't release her. Well, she wasn't going to dignify his behavior by struggling. She'd just stand here until he let her go.

But her grand plan backfired. With her eyes closed, her world was defined by her other senses. He smelled of the fresh, clean scent of the water in which he'd been swimming, and his naked flesh was cool where their arms touched. Against her body, his much larger frame felt solid and hard, and, unlike the cool skin of his arms, an intense heat radiated from him. She felt dwarfed by him, strands of her hair clinging to his tanned bare shoulders.

His breath stirred the hair near her ear, and as they stood there locked in silent confrontation, she felt his breathing change, become faster as his chest rose and fell.

"Elizabeth." He put one hand to her face and cupped her cheek, and she opened her eyes again. His face was only inches from hers, his blue eyes so compelling that she couldn't look away. His thumb caressed the line of her jaw and then he slipped it beneath her chin and exerted a light pressure, tilting her face up to his.

His features became a blur as his face moved closer, and then his lips closed over hers.

She'd kissed him before, so she really shouldn't be so

overwhelmed. His mouth was gentle but firm and insistent, warm and mobile as he explored her. His tongue traced the shape of her upper lip, then flicked along the closed line of her mouth before firmly delving between her lips, forcing them to part for him.

When her head fell back, he cradled it against his shoulder, keeping his mouth angled over hers while he plumbed the depths of her mouth. His free hand smoothed up her body from her hip to her shoulder, then firmly back down again to press her against him. She could feel him growing aroused through the thin, wet fabric between them and her body, recognizing him as surely as it had from the first, relaxed into his embrace.

Her hands had been clutching his muscled arms, prepared to push him away, but as warm pulses of fevered arousal swept through her, she slowly stroked her palms up over his shoulders, feathering delicate fingers up the back of his neck.

He shuddered. Then he tore his mouth from hers and pressed her face against his shoulder. He was panting and she hoped he wouldn't notice that she was, too.

"So you'll stay." It wasn't a question.

The self-satisfied tone in his voice had the effect of a thousand gallons of water being sprayed on a bonfire. She stiffened in his arms and, with one of the hands still around his neck, she plunged her fingers into his thick, black hair and tugged. Hard.

"Hey!" He released her immediately. "What was that for?"

"For assuming you can use sex to get me to do whatever you want."

"It worked once, didn't it?" His eyes were dark and furious.

"Now wasn't *that* the height of chivalry speaking." She knew her fair complexion was slowly becoming the vivid orange of an Arizona sunset and the knowledge only made her angrier.

"I never claimed to be a white knight," Rafe said. He thrust his own fingers through his hair and clenched his hand into a fist, his frustration evident. Then he heaved a great sigh. "I'm sorry. I don't want to get into a shouting match with you."

"Then I'll leave and you won't."

He ignored the deliberately provocative statement. "Can we start this conversation from the beginning again?"

She shrugged. Part of her wanted to get as far away from him as fast as she could. But another part, a treacherous, yearning hopefulness that she seriously despised, kept raising its own little chorus in her head, reminding her of the ecstasy she'd known in his arms and the dreams she'd woven during the long weeks since she'd seen him last. "I suppose we might."

"You're planning on keeping the baby, correct?"

She nodded. "That's correct. But I don't expect anything from you. I merely felt an obligation to inform you that you had fathered a child."

"You mean your *sister* felt that obligation," he reminded her. She bristled immediately and he held up a placatory hand. "I'm sorry. The point is, I would like you to stay in Arizona for a while as a guest in my home."

She couldn't keep the suspicion from her voice. "Why?"

He took a deep breath. "We—you and I—are going to be parents. We barely know each other. For the baby's sake, we need to learn more about each other and discuss the rearing of the child."

"This baby is mine!" Elizabeth put a protective hand over her stomach. "You wouldn't even know about it if you hadn't noticed for yourself, and you certainly weren't thrilled when you did. I told you, I don't want or need anything from you." On the verge of tears, she halted, unwilling to relive the hurt and shock she'd felt after their meeting in the restaurant, when she'd realized how little the moments in the garden house had meant to him.

"You're being unreasonable," he said. "You just walked into my life again two days ago and I learned you're carrying my child. It was a shock, and I'm sorry if I reacted badly. Elizabeth…" His voice softened, and those devastatingly direct blue eyes caught and held her gaze. "I'd like to get to know you better."

She hesitated. Staying here was a very bad idea, when all the man had to do was walk into the room, and her body began to yearn for his touch. But he was probably right. They did have some things to talk about. If she could just remember that his caresses meant nothing, that he had only kissed her in an effort to get her to weaken and agree to stay, she could handle a few days of this.

The problem was that she couldn't even remember her own name when he touched her, much less any principles.

Still, she owed this to her child. If her baby's father wanted to be involved in its life, then she was just going to have to learn to deal with Rafe Thorton. Only for the baby's sake, she reminded herself as she felt her insides automatically loosen and warm beneath the smoldering intensity of his gaze. He was only interested in her because she carried his child.

Slowly, she nodded her head. "All right. I'll stay for a few days. But you have to promise me one thing."

"Anything," he said, clearly pleased with his persuasive technique.

"No more kissing," she said.

His big body had relaxed when she'd agreed to stay. But now his muscles tensed, and his dark brows snapped together in clear displeasure. "Why?"

"Promise me." She ignored his question.

"We're attracted to each other. Don't you think it's natural for us to want to…kiss?"

The devil. She knew exactly what he was doing. His purposeful hesitation had brought all manner of memories rushing to the surface of her mind, distracting her from the conversation as she remembered the hot, wild ecstasy she'd known in his arms. Firmly, she said, "I'm not interested in casual sex. Promise me you won't start that kissing again or I'm getting the first plane out of here."

"All right," he said, and there was a grim set to his mouth. But as she watched, his lips curled into a lazy grin that curled her toes inside her shoes. "There was nothing 'casual' about the night we were together and you know it. Pretending you don't want me and I don't want you isn't going to work."

"It will have to," she insisted, though her stomach did a wild flip-flop at the look in his eyes, "or I won't stay."

It was probably just as well that he hadn't told her she'd be staying longer than a few days, Rafe reflected the next afternoon as he pulled into his driveway. He had no intention of letting her go back to Wynborough. His child was going to be a citizen of the United States of America.

He strode into the house, wondering what she'd done with herself all day. They'd agreed that she would rest and he would work as usual. He'd spent his time at the office getting things in order so that he could take a few days off.

"Hello." Elizabeth stood framed in the doorway to the kitchen.

He told himself the relief and satisfaction that rushed through him were merely a response to his concern that she might have packed and left while he was out, though she'd promised him she wouldn't. "Hello," he said. "How are you feeling?"

To his surprise, she laughed. The sound of her husky,

feminine chuckle touched chords of sexual awareness inside him, but he firmly shoved those impulses away.

"I feel fine," she said. "I'm pregnant, not ill, you know."

He smiled in return. "I know. It's just instinct, I suppose, to feel protective toward a woman carrying a child. Especially to a mere man who can't even imagine what it must be like."

Especially when that woman looks like a green-eyed angel, and she's carrying your child.

He started forward. "What did you do today? I felt badly, leaving you to your own devices, but I wanted to get my staff in order so that I could take a few days off."

"You're not working?" She sounded startled and a little dismayed.

"Not for the next few days," he said easily, though he hadn't missed her reaction. "We can't get to know each other if we don't spend time together, right?"

"I suppose you're right." She sounded less than gracious.

"Did you lounge around all day? Looks like you spent a little time in the sun."

Instinctively, she touched the tip of her nose with a fingertip, obviously making an effort to smile and match his friendly tone. "Is my complexion giving me away? I swam this morning, and I swear I sat by the pool for less than thirty minutes slathered in sunscreen, but these freckles can't be banished."

"I didn't notice the freckles. You simply have a little extra glow."

"Oh." She appeared to be at a loss for words. "I watched a chef on your telly this afternoon," she offered in what he recognized as a bid for a safer subject. "He made the most scrumptious-looking chicken dish. My mouth was watering by the time he finished. I wrote down the recipe, but I'm not really sure why—I've never cooked in my life. It looked like fun.''

Rafe chuckled. ''Most women don't consider cooking fun. They're so busy rushing around with careers and family commitments that cooking is just one more thing on the list to get finished. Where's your recipe?''

She turned and gestured behind her. ''On your kitchen counter.''

''Would you like me to teach you how to make it?''

She stared at him. ''You can cook?''

''I have become a thoroughly modern American male,'' he announced in an overly grand tone. ''I can cook, I can clean, I can provide. And all this with one hand tied behind my back, of course.''

''I'd like to learn to cook,'' she said in a somewhat hesitant tone. Then she smiled, and her eyes grew soft. ''My family will be so surprised when I get home.''

And in that moment, he promised himself that by the time she got home, she was going to think of him and smile like that, with that faraway look of familiar intimacy that made onlookers feel they'd been left outside the magic circle. But he didn't tell her any of that. ''Then I'll teach you,'' was all he said.

Over the next few days, he worked hard to make Elizabeth feel at ease. He gave her the big guest suite at the far end of the hallway from his room, and he let her have private time by the pool. He helped her learn her way around his kitchen and took her shopping for a few clothes and things to extend her stay.

She wouldn't let him hang around while she browsed the women's clothing section, which he thought was amusing. And she guarded her packages fiercely when he tried to find out what she'd bought.

"Just odds and ends," she said. They were seated in a little ice-cream café with her bags beneath the table.

"What kind of odds and ends?"

"*Ladies'* odds and ends," she said repressively.

He had to laugh. "I've seen ladies in their odds and ends before, you know. Out of them, too, come to think of it—" He stopped at the look on her face. "Magazines," he said hastily. "Men's magazines."

"Right." She made a little pout. "Here I am, buying stretchy knickers and getting fatter by the day, and you're talking about seeing women in the altogether. Thin women, no doubt."

So that was why she'd been so coy about her purchases. She was shy about buying maternity clothes. And it suddenly struck him that he was being less than a gentleman when she was probably feeling insecure enough about her body. "Elizabeth," he said. "There hasn't been a serious woman in my life in...well, ever." He leaned across the table. "And you don't have to buy *any* knickers for my benefit. I like you just fine without them."

Her face was a study in consternation. "Sh-h-h! This is hardly the place to talk about my lingerie!"

He couldn't agree more. The thought of Elizabeth as he'd seen her the night they made love, clothed only in moonlight and shadow, had its usual effect on his body. Why, he wondered, could one special woman make every one of your senses sit up and take notice while the rest... Since he'd met Elizabeth, he couldn't even remember another woman's face.

Still, he was glad he'd brought up the topic. Or pursued it. Whatever. She might insist on no kissing, but he planned to make sure she didn't forget what it had been like between them that night.

Because he fully intended to repeat it. Soon.

Her eyes were alive with wary sexual recognition and he

smiled at her, a predator's smile, lazy and content because he knew that eventually he'd get what he wanted. "Okay, we'll change the subject. What would you like to do tomorrow?"

"Cook breakfast," she said eagerly.

He stared at her for a second, then threw back his head and laughed. "Okay, we'll cook breakfast. Shall I teach you how to make French toast?"

As she nodded, it occurred to him that she was changing, absorbing American ways and independence and enjoying herself in the process.

She was never going to fit comfortably into her sheltered royal life-style again. He'd have her thoroughly Americanized soon.

The thought was more satisfying than it should have been.

A few days later, in yet another restaurant, where they'd gone at Elizabeth's request for a taste of authentic Mexican cuisine, she had the nerve to laugh at him when he suggested some of the spicier fare might not be good for the baby.

"The baby won't suffer, but I might." She smiled as she liberally splashed a hot sauce over her dish.

"Tell me about your childhood," he said, taking the bottle and setting it beyond her reach. "Not the official bio— I know that. What were you and your sisters like as children?"

A soft smile touched her lips and he wondered if she knew what her smile did to his nervous system.

"As children...well, I suppose it depends on which of us you're discussing," she said. "Alexandra is the eldest and she was a very responsible little person who took her duties much too seriously. I think she felt she had to be especially good at doing 'the royal thing' since Mummy and Daddy had lost their only son.'' The laughter in her eyes dimmed and he could see shadows of sadness. ''My parents were very loving, but there was always an awareness, if you can call it that, that our family wasn't complete. It's rather silly sounding, but true. James, my brother, was kidnapped before any of us was even born, so it wasn't as if we'd known him and missed him. It's hard to explain.''

''He was a part of your family,'' Rafe said quietly. ''I remember the kidnapping. I was about five then, I think. The whole world mourned. I remember my mother sitting in front of the television crying.''

There was a moment of silence between them. Elizabeth looked as if she was about to say something more on the topic, but then her lips firmed into a line as if she was pressing back the words.

To get her mind off the sober twist in the conversation, he said, ''Tell me about your other two sisters.''

Elizabeth's introspection vanished in the blink of an eye and she smiled that fond, intimate smile that reminded him that back in Wynborough she had a life waiting for her that didn't include him. ''Katherine is two years younger than I am. She's the quiet one most of the time.'' She grinned. ''Unless you make her mad. She was the one who put the brakes on some of our crazier stunts.''

''So you were the wild one?''

''Not quite. Serena's the baby. We all treated her like a little princess—literally—when she was small and we spoiled her terribly. If she wasn't such a sweet person, she'd be a terrible brat. Serena could twist anyone around her finger. She came up with some of the most outrageous ideas.'' She paused. ''Or shall I say that Serena came up with the ideas that got us in the most hot water?''

''I can't imagine it was too bad. All the press I ever saw portrayed you as well-behaved young ladies.''

''Oh, we were,'' she assured him. ''For the most part.''

"And the other part?"

Her eyes twinkled with mirth, and her lips parted in laughter. When she began to speak again, the little dimple in her chin deepened, and he had to resist a sudden, insane urge to reach over the table and lay his finger right in the center of that small depression.

"When I was about twelve, Serena had this great idea involving buckets of syrup and bags of feathers suspended over a doorway. Katherine tried to talk us out of it, but then she decided it might be fun and she quit whining. We did it in the stable where we could hide in the hayloft and watch. We figured we might get one of the stable lads, maybe the trainer if we were lucky."

"And did you?"

She shook her head, miming sorrow. "Unfortunately for us, my father had gone riding that day."

"You poured syrup over the *king*?" He was still steeped in his royal roots enough to be truly horrified. And he could only imagine his own father's wrath over such a stunt.

"And feathers," she added. "For what it's worth, it works magnificently."

"I just bet." He could feel the laughter bubbling up, and he let it go. When she joined in, he howled even more, mentally envisioning the reigning monarch of Wynborough covered in sticky feathers. Finally, his amusement died away to an occasional chuckle. "Remind me never to get on your sister Serena's bad side," he said.

And just that quickly the atmosphere changed. Her face sobered instantly, and she picked up her taco again. "I doubt there will ever be any occasion for you to meet," she said.

Her attitude got under his skin and before he could restrain himself, he leaned across the tiny table until he was right in her face. "As the father of your child, I'm going to be meeting *all* of your family eventually."

"Why should you?" He could tell he'd shaken her, but still she didn't back down. "It's not as if we were getting married. We barely know each other."

Her tone irritated him thoroughly, and her words annoyed him even more. "In case you haven't figured it out yet, we're going to get to know each other a whole lot better."

Four

"Fine. You want us to get to know each other, now it's your turn." Elizabeth gestured at him with her taco. He could tell he'd unsettled her when he'd spoken in that tone of voice that told her he meant every word he said, but she clearly didn't intend to let him think she was just going to *listen.* God forbid she should make it easy.

"My turn to what?" he asked.

"Tell me about your childhood."

"I only lived at home for five years before I got shipped off to boarding school," he said dismissively. "There's not much to tell."

Elizabeth set down her food and her green eyes began to flash. "I know evasion when I hear it. This getting-to-know-you bit was your idea to start with, so don't try to wriggle out of your half of the deal."

He shrugged. "There really isn't anything exciting to tell. I was sent to boarding school, went to Eton over in the U.K. from there and eventually to Oxford. That was when I decided to come to the States for further study at Harvard University.''

"You have a brother. I know him." Elizabeth was prompting him as if he were slightly slow and he sighed, having learned enough about her by now to know she wouldn't give up—or shut up—until he had satisfied her curiosity.

"Roland. I was nine when he was born. You probably know him better than I ever will. Each of us was raised virtually as an only child."

Elizabeth raised her eyebrows. "I can't imagine not being close to my family. You must have missed them terribly when you went away to school."

"No." When she turned startled green eyes on him, he realized his answer had been too immediate, too final. "My father and I are like oil and water," he said, shrugging to indicate how little it mattered. "It was a relief to everyone, I'm sure, when I was at school. When I came home on holiday, we only seemed to get on each other's nerves." An understatement of the greatest proportion. But there was no reason for her to know the rest. He'd forgotten half of it himself.

She was looking at him speculatively, and he could see that she wasn't done with the topic. So it was a surprise when she spoke again.

"So what shall we do this afternoon?"

"That depends on you," he said. "Are you tired? If you'd like to nap, we can go home." The sound of the phrase struck him forcefully. What would it be like if Elizabeth lived with him? If they really could go home together?

She wouldn't be napping alone.

The basic truth annoyed him. He wondered how many

men thought a pregnant woman was the sexiest thing they'd ever seen.

It was only that his body remembered Elizabeth's, he assured himself. It was normal to wonder if that first time had become better in retrospect than it had really been. Just because he couldn't ever remember better sex in his life was no big deal.

Then the significance of the earlier thought drowned out all others. *If Elizabeth lived with him…!* Where had that come from? True, he fully intended to marry one day, which would certainly entail sharing his home with a wife. But why was it that he could so easily picture his pregnant princess in the role?

Could there be a woman anywhere on the globe less suited to his life-style than a blueblood who'd known luxury every waking moment of her life?

The incongruity of it would be laughable if it wasn't so damned irritating. He'd spent the better part of his adult life running from his aristocratic status and here he was, about to become a father to a child who would have even more ties to royalty.

He and Elizabeth might not agree on many things, but they'd always be stuck with each other now, all because of his irresponsible behavior. For the rest of his life, he'd have royal ties that could never be broken. That much he was sure of. No child of his would be raised in the rigid, duty-demanding manner that he had been. He intended to be a warm, loving father in every way.

"I'm not tired," she said, interrupting his racing thoughts. "For the first three months all I wanted to do was sleep, but now I feel great most of the time."

The first three months.

Before he could squash the curiosity that welled, he asked, "How long was it before you realized our night together had lasting consequences?"

She slanted him an enigmatic look even though he could see the pretty pink blush deepening in her cheeks again. "You mean other than losing my virginity? *That* I realized right away."

"That wasn't what I meant and you know it." He pushed his plate aside, no longer hungry. He'd been a cad and he knew it; she didn't have to keep reminding him of how careless and thoughtless his actions had been. "When did you first suspect you were pregnant?"

She finished the last bite of her taco and set her plate aside as well, then took her sweet time dabbing at her mouth with her napkin and studiously wiping her fingers before laying it aside. She didn't look at him. Instead, her eyes were unfocused as she looked into the past. "I was worried about it right away. So I took a pregnancy test as soon as it was recommended. It confirmed my fears."

"What did you do then?" His conscience jabbed even more sharply.

Unexpectedly, she smiled. "After the first day or so of panic, I realized I was happy about it. I'm looking forward to being a mother."

"Even without a husband?"

Her smiled dimmed slightly. "Even without a husband. Though that's going to make it difficult when I tell my parents."

"Don't you think you've waited a bit long?"

Her smile grew brittle around the edges. "It's *my* baby. When and how I choose to share the news with my parents isn't your concern."

Want to bet? His jaw ached from grinding his teeth to keep from informing her that it damned well was his concern. But he knew that would be the worst thing he could say to her. A glimmer of an idea teased at the edges of his mind. If her parents didn't know yet, he might be able to use that as leverage to get her to stay. Satisfied with his own cleverness, he let it pass. "So you aren't tired. Is there anything special you'd like to do?"

She tilted her head to one side. "What I'd really enjoy is a hot air balloon ride. I read somewhere that you can take a one-hour ride over the Sonoran Desert that includes a champagne brunch—"

"No way."

"I beg your pardon?" It was her snootiest royal tone. He decided not to tell her how much it turned him on. If he did, she'd probably never use it again, just to be perverse.

"You're not going up in a hot air balloon," he said instead.

"And you would be the one making that decision?" she asked in a too-gentle tone.

"I would," he confirmed. "You're five months pregnant. They probably wouldn't take you anyway. Besides, you can't drink champagne until after the baby's born."

When she suddenly shoved her chair back from the table and stood, he was caught off-guard. "I *don't* take orders from you," she said through her teeth, both hands flat on the table. "What I do with my body and my baby is my affair and no one else's." And she spun on her heel and began to stomp out of the restaurant.

Rafe jumped to his feet. He fished money from his clip and tossed more than enough on the table to cover their meal, then surged through the tables after her.

"Go get her, buddy!" shouted some delighted onlooker from behind him.

She hadn't reached the door when he caught up to her. He didn't give her a chance to register his presence when he took her elbow and half-turned her, then swung her into his arms and began to stalk out of the eatery. Scattered clapping and scandalized laughter followed them as he carried her into the blinding midday sun. His damn sunglasses were in his shirt pocket and he couldn't get to them without setting her down, which steamed him even more.

Elizabeth was squirming and struggling. "You Neanderthal! I hated this the last time you did it! Put me down immediately."

"Not until you promise me you won't do anything stupid," he said, grimly quelling her struggles.

"Stupider than sleeping with you, you mean? That would be hard to top. That was definitely the stupidest move I ever made," she said in a bitter tone.

He set her down beside the car then, crowding her with his body to keep her from getting away as he fished his keys from his pocket. "You weren't complaining at the time," he reminded her. He yanked open her door. "Get in."

"No. I don't wish to ride with you." She folded her arms.

Rafe leaned very, very close. "Either you get in the car or you're going to be the first pregnant woman ever to get turned over a man's knee in this parking lot."

She glared at him.

He stared at her with stony implacability.

Then she turned her back on him, sliding gracefully into the passenger seat. As he slammed the door and came around to the driver's side, she said, "You don't know that."

"What?" he barked, still furious and wondering what in the hell she was talking about.

"You don't know if I would have been the first pregnant woman to get her bum smacked in this lot."

She *wasn't* going to make him smile. But he could feel the anger draining away. "No, but I'd be willing to bet on it," he said grudgingly.

There was a silence that lasted until he had pulled out

of the lot and wound his way through the streets back to the freeway.

"Look," he said, wondering why in hell he felt compelled to explain himself. "I wasn't trying to give you orders. I was concerned for your safety."

"You mean you were concerned for the baby's safety," she said quietly.

"No, that is *not* what I meant," he said. "Could you possibly quit taking exception to every word I utter? The baby is still an unknown, an abstract to me, although I know that to you it's a very real presence by now. Yes, it's important, but not as important as your safety."

"Because of your promise to my father."

He wanted to strangle her. "Fine. If that's what you want to believe, then yes. I promised your father you'd be safe with me." Another reason, far more accurate, tried to rear its head, but he ignored it. He was *not* going to let her get under his skin.

Another silence. She was looking out her window, and she had to have realized he wasn't headed for home by now, but she wouldn't look at him or speak to him.

Finally he said, "Would you like to drive out to Saguaro Lake? We could rent a canoe and paddle around the lake. It's not hot air ballooning, but it's pretty and peaceful."

She turned to face him then, and he could read surprise in her face. "That sounds lovely."

"But I'm not bringing champagne," he warned.

She gave him a small, smug smile. "I can't stand the stuff. Never drink it."

He shook his head. "You were just trying to rattle my cage back there, weren't you?"

"Maybe a little," she conceded. "May I apologize?"

"Only if you'll accept one from a Neanderthal."

She chuckled. "Done."

"Tomorrow, in Scottsdale," he said, "they celebrate the Parada del Sol. I'll take you to it if you like."

"Sol...sun? A festival for the sun?"

"Yes. The sun and wonderful climate have been good to Phoenix. The locals figure a little appreciation is in order. Did you know it's the ninth largest city in the nation?"

Her eyes widened. "But it seems so...I don't know. When I think of big cities, I think of London, New York. Everything here is golden and open, not gray and overpowering."

He nodded, relieved that she'd accepted his olive branch. "There's plenty of space here to spread out. And the climate can't be beat."

She laughed. "Growing up where we did, I suppose this is very appealing to you."

He nodded, smiling. "No rain. None of any consequence anyhow. When I wake up in the morning and walk outside, I can be assured that the sun will be there to greet me."

"You really like it here."

He took his attention from the road to glance at her. "Yes, I really do. When I first came out here, my plan was to get as far away from my father as possible. Another state farther and I'd have been in the Pacific Ocean, so I figured this was far enough."

"And has it been?" Her voice was quiet.

He sobered, reflecting. "No, not really. It's amazing that the man can still try to manipulate me from across a damned ocean."

"But you don't allow it."

"No." He shook his head firmly, positively. "There's nothing he can do or say that will affect me anymore."

"You don't say much about your mother," she observed. "The Grand Duchess has been a guest at my mother's ladies' bridge game on many occasions. She's a wicked player as I recall, having been suckered into playing against her more than once.''

Rafe nodded. ''She always enjoyed those afternoons. Having no daughters of her own, I imagine she missed female companionship.''

He spent the rest of the drive to the lake pointing out native plants and animals to her. She was amazed to see the numbers of creatures that existed in the barren, dry world of the desert where there was no water for months on end. Phoenix itself, he explained, had grown from a village into a truly disreputable outlaw town by the end of the 1800s and it wasn't until a couple of public hangings were conducted that the frontier town began to assume a semblance of civilization. After the Roosevelt Dam was created, significant power for industrial enterprise was generated, and the city began to grow and spread.

''How do you know so much about American history?'' she asked him at one point.

Rafe shrugged. ''Architecture is a field of study that often demands some knowledge of what came before in order to create a structure that reflects an area's heritage. I've always enjoyed learning about new places, and once I'd decided to settle here I was doubly interested in learning about its past.'' He chuckled. ''If you were to ask me other questions about American history, you'd find me woefully lacking in knowledge.''

She snorted. ''Somehow I doubt that.''

When they arrived at the lake, Rafe wasted no time in renting a canoe and taking her out on the water. But first he made her cover herself in sunscreen while he went into the little store and bought her a wide-brimmed hat. That creamy complexion wouldn't stand up to the strong Arizona sun, and he would never forgive himself if he let her get sunburned.

She was skittish at first when the little craft rocked slightly from side to side as he paddled.

"This is certainly different from a rowboat," she said.

"I enjoy canoeing," he said. "A canoe is easy to maneuver in the water."

She trailed her fingers over the side, letting gentle wavelets lap at her hand as she relaxed into the rocking rhythm of the little craft. "It's so peaceful out here."

He watched her from his seat at the back of the canoe as she swept a hand beneath her shoulder-length tumble of sun- touched curls, pulling them into a heavy twist atop her head, which she then anchored with a firm tug of the hat's brim. The nape of her neck was white and vulnerable and he wondered if the skin there would feel as silky under his lips as the rest of her had the night they'd made love.

Mentally, he shook his head. How could she imagine that he was never going to kiss her again?

She dipped her hand into the water again. Such a small, dainty hand. She was a small, dainty woman, more than a foot shorter than he was. She wasn't too tiny, though. As he remembered how perfectly she'd fit around him, his breath grew short and he had to look away from the languid motion of that pretty, pale hand with its long, slender fingers. Those fingers had touched him intimately, shyly at first, then more boldly when he'd shown her how much he liked it—

Damn! If he'd set out specifically to drive himself insane, he couldn't have done a much better job.

"Put sunscreen on the back of your neck," he said.

She half turned and looked over her shoulder at him, a wry smile curving her lips. "You're keen on giving orders, aren't you?"

He shrugged. "I guess it's a habit. Sorry."

She nodded her acceptance of his apology. "My father's much the same, you know. The dear man doesn't realize how autocratic he sounds at times.'' Her light laugh floated out over the lake. ''Unfortunately for him, we know there's no bite behind his bark.''

''I bet you and your sisters have him wrapped around your little fingers.''

She laughed again. ''I won't deny that he finds it hard to say no to us.''

A new thought struck him. ''Do you know yet…?'' He motioned in the general direction of her abdomen. ''Is this baby a boy or a girl?''

''I don't know. And I don't plan to ask, either.'' She lifted a hand and tucked a trailing wisp of auburn curl back beneath the hat. ''Personally, I'm hoping for a little girl I can dress in ruffles and lace.''

He grimaced. ''As long as it's healthy, I'll take whatever we get and be delighted with it.''

''I'll agree with that,'' she said.

''Although it might be nice to have some warning if it's a daughter. What I know about little girls would leave plenty of room on the head of a pin.''

She didn't answer him, but he saw her cheek dimple in a smile before she turned her head to face out over the water again.

An hour later, he tied up the canoe, and they headed back into Phoenix.

''I have to stop at the grocery store,'' he told her as they neared the suburb where his home was located.

''May I come along?'' She seemed instantly intrigued.

Her enthusiasm reminded him of his first years in the States when he'd done so many things for the first time. Things that most people took for granted, a part of everyday life that had to be done. They had no idea how exhilarating true freedom was. He knew she must be experiencing the same feelings. She had known restrictions that most people never even dreamed of. Restrictions he understood better than she might imagine.

A cage with velvet bars was still a cage.

"Of course you can come along," he said. "Have you ever been in one before?"

She shook her head. "No. There was no reason to at home. What kinds of things do we need to buy?"

We. Such a simple little word. How could it change so many things? He wondered if she even realized she'd used it as he answered.

"Breakfast foods. Lunch meats. The ingredients for the chicken dish you wrote down. Fruits and vegetables. Cleaning supplies—"

"Stop!" She was smiling. "I get the picture."

She wanted to push the cart at first, simply for the novelty of it all. Then she wanted him to explain the price comparisons and the meaning of the dietary listings on the back. What would normally have taken him less than thirty minutes became a two-hour tour of the grocery market.

When they finally had finished and he'd loaded the last of the groceries into the back of the truck, he swung into the driver's seat and snagged his seat belt. Automatically he glanced over at her. Then he frowned.

"You shouldn't be wearing your seat belt like that."

"Like what?" She glanced down at herself, then back at him, clearly mystified.

He leaned across the seat, snagging his fingers in the lap belt she'd pulled over her belly and tugging it down beneath the bulge of his child to rest across her hips. "I've seen warnings about this. Pregnant women should be careful not to position the belt too high. If there was an accident, the belt could harm the baby."

"Oh." Her voice was slightly breathless.

With sudden, shocking clarity Rafe became aware of how close they were. His breath stirred the copper curls

about her ears, and the arm he'd draped over the back of
the seat was very nearly an embrace around her shoulders.
His fingers, where he'd hooked them beneath the seat belt,
rested against soft feminine flesh. He'd pulled the belt
down as he'd spoken so that now his hand was practically
nested in the warm pocket where her thighs met her body.
His fingers were held firmly against her by the constriction
of the seat belt.

She froze.

So did he, largely because his entire being was caught
up in the battle raging inside him: the gentlemanly part of
him that knew he should move away versus the purely male
impulse to extend his fingers down and brush over the sensitive flesh he knew lay just beyond his loosely curled hand.
It was a toss-up as to which one would win.

And then she took the choice from him.

Slowly, her hand came up and snared his wrist, her small
fingers braceleting his hard male sinew, not even meeting
around the thickness of his arm. It was clearly a signal to
halt. She didn't tug his hand away, though, only turned her
head and tilted up her chin to look at him with wide, questioning eyes.

The desire to lower his head and take her lips was nearly
too much for him to resist. But he'd promised her. No kissing.

Damn that promise!

Holding her gaze, he slowly, slowly slid his hand from
beneath the seat belt fabric, caressing her flesh with the
back of his hand as he withdrew, moving higher to let his
knuckles lightly skim over a nipple, which elicited a swiftly
indrawn breath from her. Not a moan, but not far from it,
either.

Without a word, he slid his arm from behind her and
turned his attention to starting the truck and pulling out of
the lot. She didn't speak the whole way home and neither

did he, though he was hard-put to contain the elation dancing around inside him.

She'd said no more kissing, but she hadn't said a word about touching—and she hadn't objected just now to what had been a whole lot more intimate than some kisses he'd experienced.

What in the world had she been thinking? Or not thinking?

Washing up before joining Rafe to work on the recipe she'd copied from the television, Elizabeth held a cool face-cloth to cheeks that burned at the very memory of his hard, hot fingers pressed firmly against her body. If she'd been naked, those fingers would have been nestled in the curling hair that protected her most private flesh.

If you'd been naked he would have been doing a whole lot more with those fingers.

She groaned and flopped the sopping cloth over her entire face. She was an imbecile. An imbecile ruled by her hormones. And she didn't mean pregnancy hormones, either. She couldn't even be in the same room with the man without her heart beating faster and her mind conjuring up vivid pictures of him embracing her, his body hard and demanding against her soft, yielding one.

Staying here in his home was the dumbest thing she'd done since…well, since she'd slept with a perfect stranger and gotten herself pregnant.

But in her heart she didn't consider Rafe a stranger. Not then and not now. They might not know each other well, but her body and her heart knew all they needed to know to assure her that he was the only man she'd ever want.

She snatched the cloth off her face and stared at herself in the bathroom mirror.

Oh, no. No, no, no, no, *no!* She was *not* in love with Rafe Thorton.

He didn't want her, at least not in any way other than the purely physical, and she'd *promised* herself she wasn't going to weave any more foolish romantic fantasies around him.

But oh, it was hard to make her heart listen to her common sense. All her life she'd dreamed of a man who would breach the fortress of security around her and carry her off to a world where she could be just another ordinary person. These easy-flowing hours the past few days had given her more contentment than she'd known in her entire life.

She loved living in a single-story home with only a few bedrooms as opposed to an entire wing of bedroom suites with drafty hallways half a kilometer long. She loved the casual atmosphere in which one simply drove one's car out of the garage and went to the market instead of calling a chauffeur. She loved everything about the life Rafe had created for himself, and that was part of the problem.

She couldn't let his life-style confuse her. She couldn't fall for him simply because he embodied the kind of life she'd always longed for in her most secret heart.

But this experience had been good for her in some ways. She was determined that her child wasn't going to be raised in a hothouse environment. She wasn't blind to the fact that she might always need discreet security, but she was determined to make as normal a life for her baby as she could.

And that didn't include being escorted everywhere she went every minute of the day. So far, Rafe had treated her exactly in the hothouse-flower way that her own parents always had. He might be content with his lifestyle, but he clearly didn't think it was right for her.

Before she'd known who he was, she'd woven the most ridiculous romantic fantasies about her mysterious lover. Now, she could only thank heaven that she'd gotten wise.

Of course she didn't love him.

She repeated that to herself the whole way out to the kitchen where he was waiting for her.

"Ready for another lesson in preparing American cuisine?" Rafe stood at the counter, where he'd assembled what looked like half his kitchen's worth of cooking equipment.

"Ready for another lesson in preparing any kind of cuisine," she said lightly, walking across the room to join him. It was hard to meet his eyes after the thoughts that had just been running around in her brain, so she concentrated on the items before her.

Without thinking about what she was doing, she opened the cabinet doors beneath his sink and withdrew a dishpan, drainer, dish soap and a cleaning cloth. Automatically she began to fill the dishpan with hot water.

"What are you doing?"

She glanced at him. "Getting out the cleaning things so we can get rid of the mess as we make it."

"Since when does a princess think about cleaning up? Don't you have servants for the menial tasks?"

His tone had been merely curious, but it still made her bristle. "You were raised much as I was. You already know the answer to that."

"But I wasn't," he said. "Remember? I lived at school most of my childhood. And, believe me, one learned to clean up at those venerable institutions."

"Kitchen duty for breaking the rules?" She smiled, determined to keep a civil distance between them. After all, he was her host.

"Occasionally." He grimaced. "Bathroom duty was worse."

"Infinitely." Genuine amusement lit her eyes. "Although there's a tremendous satisfaction to be gained from seeing porcelain and steel gleam through your efforts."

"And how would you know that?" He raised his eyebrows skeptically. "I can't imagine you scrubbing toilets in the family castles."

She chuckled. "I can't quite see that myself. But for the past three years, I've volunteered at a children's hospital."

"And they asked you to clean their bathrooms?" He was grinning.

"I did anything that was necessary," she said, her face growing serious. "It would be a terribly bad example for others to see me pick and choose tasks as if I were too important for some."

He didn't want to let her see how impressed he was by her attitude. By all rights, she should be a spoiled, demanding brat, but she wasn't. In fact, she was one of the most conscientious, sensible women he'd met in a long time, he thought, recalling her concern when she thought her parents might be worrying about her.

But all he said was, "Good point. Now, are you ready to make your first jen-yoo-wine American entrée?"

She laughed. "Ready."

It wasn't until later that the fragile truce ended.

They'd put together the casserole she'd chosen, which thankfully had been pretty straightforward. While he'd become a credible cook since he'd been forced to feed himself, Rafe was under no illusions about the limitations of his culinary skills.

As she'd insisted, they cleaned up the dishes as they went so there wouldn't be a huge mess at the end. He liked the idea since he usually had a mini-disaster area in his kitchen after any cooking effort.

As she passed him the final mixing bowl to dry and put away, she folded the dishtowel over its bar. They worked well together, he realized. That would be helpful after they were married, one area in which they could be relatively compatible.

After they were married. A few weeks ago—hell, a few *days* ago—he'd have thought someone who mentioned marriage and Rafe Thorton in the same sentence was insane.

But everything was different now. When had he realized that? So, okay, maybe she wasn't what he'd envisioned when he'd entertained hazy, half-formed thoughts of a wife and family. But she was carrying his child and that made all the difference. *That and the way she goes up in flames every time you touch her.*

It would be best to get things settled between them quickly, he decided. He clattered the bowl into the cabinet and closed the door, then turned and walked to her. She merely looked at him with puzzled, wary eyes when he took her hands.

"Elizabeth. Marry me." It might not have been the most romantic proposal in the world, but it wasn't as if they were in love or anything. This was strictly a necessity in his eyes, to give his child a name.

"No, thank you." She spoke as calmly as if she were declining a second helping at a meal. She slipped her hands free of his and linked them together at her waist.

There was a long, taut silence while his brain processed the fact that she'd refused his offer. *She'd refused him!* Summoning a calm tone that he was proud matched her cool little voice, he said, "No, thank you? Any possibility you'd expand on that?"

She hesitated. "You do me a great honor with your offer," she said formally, politely, not meeting his eyes. "But I have no wish to marry solely to provide a family unit for this child. You and I lead very different lives."

"That we do," he said grimly, annoyed at the way she'd reduced his proposal to a mere matter of convenience, conveniently ignoring the fact that he'd done exactly the same thing a few minutes ago. "And there's no way I'm ever going back overseas, not for you, not for anyone."

"I didn't ask you to!" Her tone wasn't so calm anymore. Pivoting, she flounced to the other side of the counter and stood staring out the window with her back to him.

The unspoken dismissal broke the thin threads by which he'd been holding together his temper. "You'd like that, wouldn't you, if I'd fall into line like a good little subject and—"

She whirled. "If you were a good little subject, you'd be even more objectionable than you are now!"

"Well, you aren't exactly my first choice, either." Her belligerent words had stung. "My plan was to marry a home-grown American girl who doesn't have a drop of blue blood or aspirations to a title when I was good and ready. A *princess* doesn't exactly fill the bill."

"Good!" Her face was flushed, and unless he was mistaken, her eyes held the sheen of tears. "Then you have no problem accepting that you did the honorable thing and proposed and I chose to decline."

"Fine!" He was as mad as she was now. Then he thought about what he'd just said. "Hold it. *Not* fine. My child isn't going to be born a bastard."

Her brows snapped together. "That's a nasty word and I don't appreciate you applying it to our child."

"Why not? Other people will."

One of the tears that had been swimming around in her eyes broke the dam and spilled down her cheek. "They wouldn't dare."

"Of course they would. You know how people love good gossip. Just imagine the fodder an illicit liaison between royals of Wynborough and Thortonburg would provide them—" The look on her face stopped him midsentence.

A moment of silence as pregnant as the woman before him hung in the air between them.

"You weren't going to tell them, were you?" A part of him wondered why it bothered him so much. After all, it would get him out of an inconvenient marriage and ensure that he didn't get sucked back into his father's title-seeking sphere again. But a bigger part of him rejected the idea that his child wouldn't bear his name.

"You weren't even going to tell them," he accused again. "You planned to go home to Wynborough with this baby in your belly and never tell your parents who the father was, didn't you?"

"Why not? It makes sense." Her face was still flushed with anger. "Neither of us wants to marry the other. You weren't planning on becoming a father now. There's no reason to involve yourself in my life."

"No reason?" He was so mad, he had to clench his fists to keep from reaching for her. "You're going to bear my child in a matter of months. *My child.* Not that of some anonymous man who you can dismiss for his rather negligible role in the conception." He stalked around the counter until he was only inches from her, leaning forward to speak right into her startled, defiant face. "This baby is going to be legitimate if I have to tie you up and fly to Las Vegas for a quickie wedding."

Her eyes rounded. "You wouldn't dare."

"Try me," he invited. "And while I'm at it, I'll get on the telephone and call your parents. I'm sure your father would be pleased to know I'd done the right thing by you."

Her face drained of color. "You *can't* tell my parents," she said. She half turned away from him. "This baby can't be—" She stopped abruptly and put a hand out toward the counter, and he saw her sway. "I feel…" He didn't wait for any more. He'd never seen anyone faint, and he wasn't going to start now. Taking a half step that brought him to her side, he drew her into his arms.

She gave a startled squeak that trailed off into a moan, but she didn't fight him, merely laid her head against his chest. After a moment, he led her into the living room and laid her on the couch, then placed a pillow under her feet.

She moaned again, but this time there was an element of relief in the sound. The band of tension squeezing his throat relaxed marginally and he nudged her over gently to make space to perch beside her.

"Can I get you anything?" His voice was deep with concern, and he didn't care if she noticed.

"No, I'll be all right." She groped for his hand. "Just— don't go."

Her small fingers found his and clung, and he was astonished by the force of the emotion that roared through him. His throat grew tight again and he had to clear it roughly before he squeezed her fingers and said, "I'm right here."

Long moments passed. He watched her closely. Her eyes were closed, dark silky lashes lying soft against her cheeks, and gradually a hint of pink crept back to replace her pallor. Her clutch on his hand lessened. Even so, he made no move to release her.

Finally, her eyelashes fluttered and slowly her eyelids rose to reveal deep, mysterious emerald pools that swam with emotions he couldn't name. "I'm sorry," she said quietly.

"Don't be. I'm the one who should be sorry." Disgusted with himself, he looked away from her. "I should be treating you more carefully—"

"I'm not sorry about almost fainting," she said, smiling. "I meant I was sorry to have gotten into a shouting match with you. I'm not usually such a shrew."

"You have nothing to apologize for," he told her firmly.

"You weren't the only one shouting, in case you hadn't noticed."

"I'd noticed," she said in a dry tone. Then her face sobered. "I'm also sorry for treating your feelings and wishes as if they count for nothing. I don't want to deny you your child."

"We can talk about that later," he said, anxious not to let more discord mar the day. She still might not understand that marriage wasn't negotiable; it was a *fact,* but there was nothing to be gained by antagonizing her again right now.

An odd odor assailed his nostrils, almost as if something was burning—

"The casserole!" they shouted in unison as Rafe bolted for the kitchen.

Five

Marrying him was out of the question.

As she applied mascara to her lashes several days later, Elizabeth felt a definite kick just beneath the right side of her rib cage. Laying her hand gently over the swell of her belly, she thought again of the father of the baby growing within her.

Again? That was a bit of a lie, she thought ruefully. Rafe Thorton had been in her thoughts since the night he'd taken her into the garden house and he hadn't left yet.

What was she going to do? He hadn't sounded as if he was kidding when he'd told her she would marry him. Not kidding at all. Even though she knew he didn't love her, knew she was one of the last women on earth he'd ever take as wife of his own free will, he planned to marry her to provide his child with a legitimate heritage.

An admirable intent, certainly. It would be even more admirable if she wasn't the one he was intent on marrying.

Rafe's intense blue eyes materialized in her mental meanderings and she groaned. If only the darned man wasn't so appealing. Irresistible. Adorable… He'd die if he heard *that* description, she thought with a soft chuckle. But the chuckle dried in her throat when she recalled the sharp words they'd exchanged.

Since their last confrontation they'd been as polite as casual acquaintances, avoiding anything the least bit controversial. He'd taken her to the Parada del Sol, they'd watched the beginning of a hot air balloon race and, at dawn the day before he'd driven her into the desert to watch the sun rise. He'd been gracious, friendly…and as remote as a distant moon.

There was no way they could marry. Aside from the attraction that seemed to charge the air between them, they had nothing in common. He'd been independent for more than a decade, had lived in the States long enough to be truly an American now. She was enjoying her experience in the country immeasurably, but she'd never known the kind of freedom these people took for granted.

She loved and respected her family. Though Rafe had said little about his own, she had gotten the distinct impression he wasn't particularly fond of his nearest kin.

She'd been raised with an exceptionally fine liberal arts education that had prepared her for no practical work. Rafe had used his education to carve out an amazingly successful career for himself.

No, marriage was definitely out of the question, regardless of what Rafe had said about Las Vegas.

Las Vegas! Oh, how she'd love to see it. Serena had been married there a short time ago in one of those "have to see it to believe it" chapels, as her sister had put it, laughing gaily. Elizabeth had gotten on the Internet this afternoon and looked up some information on the town that had risen in the middle of the Nevada desert. It certainly looked like a fascinating place and she was determined to visit it one day.

The baby stirred beneath her palm and she rubbed her hand over her belly again, sighing. The next few months couldn't go fast enough. Not only was she aching with the need to hold her child in her arms, she was nearly as excited at the thought of having a waistline again.

It was bad enough that Rafe had to provoke her into acting like a fishwife, but even worse that she felt so fat and unattractive around him. She longed for her former slim figure, the figure she'd had when they'd first met and he hadn't known who she was.

A knock on the door of her suite startled her and she nearly dropped the mascara wand she was still holding.

"Are you ready?"

"Almost. Just give me a moment."

Hastily she finished adding the little makeup she normally wore and picked up her jacket and bag from where she'd laid them on the bed. Opening the door, she stepped into the hallway to face Rafe and her breath caught in her throat.

He was so handsome. In a simple cream shirt and khaki pants, he managed to look better to her than other men did in a tux. He smiled when he saw her, and the deep creases his dimples made flashed in his lean cheeks.

"Ready to go?" he asked her.

"Ready." As he took her elbow and escorted her through the house she added, "Though it might be nice to know where we're headed."

"I told you it's a surprise," he said, grinning smugly. He led her into the garage and held the door of the sleek Mercedes she'd discovered he kept in addition to his serviceable truck. "You'll just have to wait and see."

He drove her northeast through the city to Scottsdale Municipal Airport where he apparently already had arranged a flight. But when they walked onto the airfield, Elizabeth stopped and resisted his hand on her arm urging her forward.

"That's a *small* plane," she said in dismay. And it was. Though she'd often taken puddle-jumpers back and forth between Wynborough and the U.K., this plane looked like a life-sized toy. Two men standing outside the single door waved when they caught sight of Rafe and again he urged her forward.

"It's a twin-engine and it's bigger than some private planes," Rafe said. "If I had a pilot's license, we could have taken a two-seater."

"And how many seats are there in this?" she asked apprehensively.

"Four. That's the pilot and co-pilot waiting for us."

"It takes two men to fly something this small?"

"Not normally, no. This usually is only used for pleasure tours around the city."

"Ah-hah! So we're going somewhere outside Phoenix."

By then they had reached the waiting pilots, and after quick introductions Elizabeth was led up a very small, very steep flight of steps into the tiny cabin.

It was beautifully appointed, far nicer than she'd expected. Served her right for forgetting that while Rafe might act like nothing more than an American businessman, he had a small fortune at his disposal.

As she settled into the comfortable leather seat she asked, "Now do I get to know where we're going?"

"Actually, we have two destinations," Rafe told her. "We'll only be doing a flyover of the first one, though. Just settle back and enjoy."

"Settle back and enjoy," she grumbled. But the anticipation dancing in his eyes seduced her into an equally good humor, and as the little plane rose and circled to the north, she relaxed and enjoyed the receding view of the city and the interesting combination of desert and mountain around it.

"That's Flagstaff," Rafe told her a few minutes later. "And in just a minute, if you look out your window, you'll see the highest point in the state of Arizona, Humphrey's Peak."

"Who was Humphrey?"

He laughed. "I don't have a clue. See, I told you I didn't know everything about this country."

She continued to gaze out her window at the peaks and valleys they passed, and then they flew over a densely wooded forest. "Where are we now?" she asked.

"Just keep watching." Rafe unbuckled his seat belt and came to kneel at her side. "In another minute or two, you should be able to see it."

"See *what?*" She was intensely aware of his big warm body so close, the clean smell of newly showered man and cologne. To distract herself she angled an elbow at his ribs, but he dodged away, chuckling. He was impossible to resist in this mood. And she was so tired of forcing herself to ignore the pull of sensual promise that his intense eyes promised.

"Now look," he said in her ear and she turned her head and peered out her window, resolutely ignoring the shiver that rushed down her spine at the sensation of hot breath bathing her sensitive earlobe.

"Oh! It's—it's incredible. Beautiful. *Huge.*" Below their little plane the Grand Canyon yawned wider and deeper than she'd ever thought possible. She turned to him, overwhelmed. "Oh, Rafe, thank you! I hadn't expected to get to see this during my trip."

His face was only inches away, his broad shoulders and arms bracketing her seat and creating a small haven of intimacy. Before she allowed herself to think too much about it, she leaned forward and brushed a soft kiss over his lips.

Then she quickly turned her head and looked out the window again.

"What happened to the 'no kissing' edict?" he asked in her ear. His voice was deep and seductive, and she took deep breaths until the urge to turn back into his arms subsided enough to control.

She cleared her throat. "I made the rule. I can break it if I like," she said.

He laughed yet again and warm breath played over her ear. Slowly his arms came around her from behind, drawing her back against his chest, surrounding her with heat and scent and the feel of his hard forearms clasped over her belly. Her breasts rested against his arms and her breath began to come faster as desire rushed through her.

To distract herself from her body's messages, she concentrated on the glowing colors of the canyon and the distinct striations in the rock that she knew marked different periods of Earth's geological history dating back millions of years.

The plane banked to the left, turning away from the morning sun and heading west as they followed the shining ribbon that was the mighty Colorado River winding through the canyon. The canyon narrowed, then widened again and finally a huge, gleaming lake appeared beneath them.

"That's Lake Mead," Rafe explained. "It's man-made, a result of the Hoover Dam, which you'll see in a minute."

And then the dam was past, and they were turning due west once again. The flat plain of a desert spread below them and in the distance some sort of city rose out of the desert like a mirage—

"Where are we?" Suspicion tinged her tone.

"Don't recognize Tinseltown? I wish I'd been able to bring you in at night, but we'd have had to miss the canyon then." Casually, Rafe withdrew his arms and straightened, returning to his seat to buckle himself in as if he was completely unaffected by the embrace in which he'd been holding her.

"Las Vegas! We're going to Las Vegas?" She didn't know whether to be apprehensive or excited. It couldn't be a coincidence that he'd brought her here when they'd been dancing around the topic of marriage for days. Could it?

"It's a unique place."

"My sister was married here recently," she informed him. "I'm not sure this is such a good idea."

Rafe shrugged his shoulders. "I thought you'd enjoy spending the day here. But if not, we can just refuel and head back home."

"No, it's not that. I'm sure I would enjoy it. But..." There was no way to say it without sounding paranoid and silly. *I'm afraid you'll make me marry you?* Too ridiculous for words. She was entirely too suspicious for her own good.

As if he'd read her mind, Rafe laid a hand gently over hers. "You'll like it, I promise," he said. "I would never make you do something that you didn't want to do."

And so she found herself in a taxi less than half an hour later, heading through the glaring sunshine to a city that never slept.

He took her to Caesar's first, leading her through the casinos to the huge shopping plaza beyond. They lunched at the Italian restaurant in the center and she marveled at the sky that changed from dawn to dusk, through night and back to day again in less than an hour.

At the Mirage, Rafe had gotten tickets to a special showing of Siegfried and Roy's magic show that included unbelievable special effects as well as their trademark white tigers and other animals. When the show ended, Rafe escorted her to the front desk, where the mention of his name produced quick and efficient service in a private office.

Pocketing the key he had received, Rafe smiled at her

startled expression as he led her to the elevator. "Well, you can't expect to go all day without rest, can you? I got a suite so that you could take a nap if you like."

The concierge attendant led them to their room and didn't blink an eye when Rafe told him they had no luggage. "Very good, sir," was the man's only reaction before he shut the door, leaving the two of them standing in the foyer of the spacious suite.

"I'm impressed," she said lightly, trying to conceal the sudden attack of nerves that assailed her. "Don't they usually reserve these for the folks who drop a significant bundle with their establishment every year?"

"There are ways around that." Rafe prowled the room like the great tigers they'd just seen, opening doors and cabinets. He gestured. "The bedroom's through here. Why don't you lie down for a while?"

She *was* tired, even if she hated to admit it to him. The day had been full of fun and excitement and a lot of walking—more than she was accustomed to, if she was honest. While she hadn't gained a great deal of weight yet, the eight pounds she'd added to her slender frame made a difference and her feet were aching.

"What are you going to do?" she asked. The thought of sleeping in the single bedroom of the suite while Rafe prowled the living area made her feel vulnerable in a not entirely reasonable way. Which was stupid, she reflected, when she slept in his home every night.

Still, their bedroom suites were at opposite ends of the hallway in his house and she didn't even see him after dinner unless she so chose.

"I'll find something to occupy an hour or two," he assured her. "I'll go downstairs and gamble away enough money to make our hosts happy. I'll be back near six, though, because I want to show you the volcano outside the hotel and then watch the pirate ship battle the British down at Treasure Island. You have to see it to believe it. Somewhere in there, we'll get some dinner."

"That sounds lovely." She smiled at him across the room and his gaze seemed to snare her so that she couldn't look away. His eyes were deeply blue and compelling, as if he were willing her toward him. The moment stretched and shimmered between them.

In a deep, rough voice, he said, "Lovely enough for another kiss?"

Every nerve in her body sprang to life. She wanted to kiss him and she didn't. Stalling, she said, "Is that the price for today?"

He was already starting across the room. "No price tag on the day," he said. "This would be purely a bonus for extraordinary service."

He was directly in front of her now, and she had to tilt her head back to see his face. "Well," she said, "I guess you should get a bonus. It's been a pretty spectacular day." She lowered her gaze to the open neck of the shirt he wore, waiting for him to take the lead.

"But I'm not allowed to kiss you, remember?" He was breathing faster and his eyes were even more intense than usual, narrowed and brilliant with desire, but there was indulgent humor in his voice.

"I'd forgotten," she said. "In that case..." Taking a deep breath for courage, she stepped closer and lifted her hands to his shoulders to balance herself, then stood on tiptoe. "Thank you," she whispered and pressed a soft kiss to his smiling lips, momentarily molding her mouth to his firm, warm one.

His hands came up to her wrists, holding her in place, and he made a sound of approval deep in his throat. Then before she could back away, his mouth shifted against hers, hardening in demand. The kiss became his instead of hers and she whimpered at the surge of sensation that tightened her body with a desire she'd been suppressing for days.

Her hands gripped his shoulders and he slid his own down from her wrists, traveling over the curves of her body as he held her mouth with his, demanding a response that she gave without thinking, without hesitation. His thumbs briefly caressed her hipbones, still evident despite the mound of his child in her womb, and then he gripped her soft curves, pulling her against him and shocking her system with the hard warm promise of his big body.

This, she thought hazily, was what she'd remembered from their first meeting, this magnetic pull that erased conscious decision and attracted her to him. Opposite charges creating a bond. The hard probe of his tongue sought out every response from her own; his muscled arms and shoulders blocked out the light as he loomed over her, making her feel small and fragile. Against her belly, taut masculine flesh swelled, and when he lifted her off her feet and his arousal found the hidden pocket of warmth at her thighs, her startled intake of breath matched the groan wrenched from his throat.

This was the man about whom she'd woven her foolish fantasies, the man whose skillful hands and hard body had claimed her, making it impossible for her to forget him. She had to remember…what? Her distracted thoughts whirled in her head under the sensual onslaught, and as desire mounted it became less and less crucial that she recall what her brain was struggling to bring into focus.

His hands stroked restlessly up and down her back; he no longer needed to bind her to him. One big palm slipped around her rib cage to cover a breast. Even through her clothing, his thumb sought out the tender peak, circling her nipple until it stood out in bold relief, the contact sending arrows of arousal straight to the aching flesh between her legs. Restlessly she pressed herself closer. As if he recognized her need, he slipped one hard thigh between hers, pressing upward so that she was firmly lodged against his leg, the small press and release of his muscled thigh spiraling her closer and closer to the reckless edge of passion.

Finally he released her mouth, sliding his lips along her jaw and down to the vulnerable flesh beneath her chin, sucking and licking, flicking a relentless rhythm over the tender skin as he worked his way down to the upper swells of her breasts. He nuzzled aside the button-front shirt she wore, but eventually the fabric frustrated him and he abandoned his efforts, simply closing his lips over the taut nipple shielded from his view and suckling strongly.

She gave a high, smothered cry as the shock reverberated through her system, and though she wouldn't remember it later, her back arched and her hands came up to plunge into his thick hair and hold him closer. Her fingers flexed and kneaded his scalp and he dragged one hand away from her back to begin working at the buttons of her blouse until he'd freed enough that he could pull the fabric aside and lift her breast free of her bra.

His mouth on her bare flesh was yet another shocking wonder. How could she have forgotten this? Logical thought receded and she gave herself to the hot magic flowing between them, her knees giving way so that she sank to the thick carpet, pulling him down as she went. Within minutes, they were sprawled in a needy tangle of limbs struggling to remove clothing even as they explored newly bared skin.

When he had removed the bikini panties that still fit beneath the bulge of her belly, Rafe sat back on his heels for a long moment, studying the changes in her form since the last time they'd been together. Under his intense scrutiny she blushed, raising a knee and covering her breasts with her arms.

He gave a quiet chuckle, then stretched his length beside

her, propping himself on an elbow and laying a hot, hairy leg over hers, gently but inexorably tugging until she relaxed her arms from their defensive posture. Bending his head, he touched a light kiss to the crest of the nearest breast.

"You are so beautiful," he said almost reverently. "Before, in the dark, I wished I could see you better." He placed his open palm at her throat and slowly smoothed it in a long, slow glide down the midline of her body, dragging it through the valley between her breasts, down past her navel and finally stopping when his big palm covered the place where their child was sheltered.

She raised her own hands to his broad, bare shoulders, exploring the muscular flesh with gentle fingers, running her hands up to cradle his stubbled jaw, marveling at the differences in a man's body. Oh, she was no naive schoolgirl. She knew a lot about what happened between men and women, courtesy of many gossipy, giggly late-night sessions with the girlfriends her parents made sure were a part of their daughters' lives.

And she'd had that one wondrous, magical night with Rafe...when everything had seemed dusted with magic and moonlight, and her inhibitions had slipped away into the shadows under his expert handling.

He leaned over her then, kissing her deeply, caressing her silky skin until she was arching against him, small whimpers escaping each time his hand ventured into sensitive territory. She didn't want to talk, didn't want to think. She only wanted to feel, to savor every brush of his fingers, every inch of his body against hers.

His hand slipped lower and lower over her belly and into the warm thatch of curls below, and she gave a strangled cry of shock as he deliberately pushed on. One long finger slid between her soft folds, spreading the moisture he found there in ever-widening circles until her nails were digging into his shoulders and she tugged at his lean hips, trying to drag him closer.

He answered her wordless plea with his body, moving atop her and settling himself in the space she willingly made between her thighs. She could feel him, throbbing and silky against her belly and she slipped a hand between them, needing to feel the proof of his desire for her. He groaned as she cupped him and his hips thrust involuntarily at her, then he captured her hand and kissed her fingers before anchoring both hands above her head with his own.

Slowing, he drew back, allowing his heavy flesh to find its home between her thighs, nudging at her gently but insistently until the slick channel he'd prepared for himself opened. He thrust forward in one strong stroke then, pushing into her in the ultimate joining while he kissed her again and again, hard, stinging kisses that spoke more clearly than words of the control he was exerting. She wriggled beneath him to lodge him even more firmly in place, then rocked her hips lightly, savoring the slippery movement of flesh in flesh.

Looking up at his chiseled features, she felt her heart swell with love. It was ridiculous to deny it. Oh, she might never tell Rafe, but it was silly to pretend she didn't love him, had begun to lose her heart when their eyes had met across a ballroom. She'd loved him since that night, the one night he'd been all hers without any of this baggage between them muddying feelings and relationships.

He kissed her again as if he would never stop, and she closed her eyes, wanting to impress every memory into her mind, to save these precious moments for the long, lonely days that she feared were ahead. She didn't know what the rest of her life might hold; she only knew that Rafe wouldn't be there, and she doubted she'd ever feel about another man the way she felt about him. It had happened for her parents—mutual, instantaneous love that defied social class and expectations, and she'd been raised to respect the sacred joining of two souls. Marriage shouldn't happen unless there was love between the parties involved.

Rafe drew back, then pushed forward again, and the sensations his body produced where he moved within and over her were so exquisite that she couldn't prevent the soft sound of need that escaped.

"I thought of you." His voice was a rough confession in her ear. "So many times, I nearly hopped on a plane and came to find you."

It was the first time she'd had any indication that he might have been as affected by their night of lovemaking as she had been, and it was the most powerful aphrodisiac she'd ever known.

"I wish you had," she whispered. Then she shifted her legs higher, clasping his lean waist, and gave herself to the moment. As he began to move heavily against her, she turned her face into his chest and moved in counterpoint, meeting his thrusts. He unclasped her wrists and drew his hand down to brace himself, and she laid her palms over the smooth muscles of his shoulders, feeling the heat and sweat, feeling a throbbing tension drawing taut at the point where his body slammed into her over and over. She'd noticed an increased sensitivity in her breasts and other places as her pregnancy progressed, and the rhythmic thrusting was quickly more than she could take.

With an incoherent cry, she convulsed in his arms, writhing as climax ripped through her. Rafe followed almost immediately, as if he'd been waiting for her and she wrapped her arms around him, dimly feeling the pulses of his own release flooding warmly within her, awareness slowly returning as ecstasy receded into a lethargic satisfaction.

She yawned against his chest and felt a chuckle rumble

through him. He started to shift away, but she wrapped her arms around his shoulders. "Stay."

"I'm planning to." He lifted a hand and smoothed her hair back from her face, lingered over the curve of her cheek. "But I have to move. I don't want to hurt you or the baby."

Reluctantly, she relaxed her grip, hating the moment when he pulled away from her, but nearly as quickly he slid to her side and shifted her so that he lay on his back with her cuddled against him. His arm was hard around her and the hair on his chest was tickling her nose. She'd never been so content in her entire life. Heaving a sigh that made him chuckle again, she closed her eyes and slipped into sleep, safe in his embrace.

Two hours later, Rafe stepped out of the shower and wrapped a towel around his waist. Quietly he walked through the bedroom, and, as the knock he'd been expecting sounded at the door, he quickly pulled it open before the man standing on the other side could knock again.

"The things you requested, sir," the valet said. The man pushed a garment cart with several bagged items hanging from it into the room, then efficiently dealt with the bags piled on its bottom rack. As Rafe watched, all kinds of toiletries and accessories appeared: a shaving kit, a selection of makeup, the ladies' maternity underclothes he'd specified, perfume and men's cologne and more, right down to a handbag and pretty, low-heeled sandals for his sleeping beauty.

Rafe signed the bill the man discreetly presented, adding a generous tip before he ushered him out, closing the heavy door quietly. Elizabeth was still sleeping on the bed where he'd carried her after their lovemaking, and he suspected she needed a little more rest before their evening began. She was going to be hard enough to handle when she found out what he had planned; no point in having her tired and cranky as well.

He'd sworn he would never wind up like his parents, and now he was doing nearly the exact same thing.

The bitter thought tore through his mind and he felt compelled to defend his decision. He was not doing the same thing his parents had done. Well, not exactly. His parents' marriage had been a power deal and his mother hadn't been pregnant at the time of the ceremony. Although it certainly hadn't been long before she was.

The thought boggled the mind. He couldn't imagine two people less likely to indulge in hot, sweaty, draining but delightful bouts of sex than his parents. Victor and Sara were the least passionate people he'd ever met.

Unless you were talking prestige or finances, he thought with a bitterness that hadn't subsided over the years. His father lived to ingratiate himself with the royalty of every European nation that hadn't gotten rid of the archaic idea of a ruling class. Anyone who dared to thwart Victor in one of his never-ending attempts to link himself with yet another royal name found out just how passionate he could get.

As a child, Rafe had learned quickly that protocol and etiquette were the keys to success in his home. One didn't run to one's mother for a kiss upon her return from a trip, or cry over a skinned knee. His father's favorite phrase, without doubt, was "stiff upper lip."

And Rafe was damned if his child was ever going to hear it.

He pulled on the black evening trousers and slipped into the shirt, fastening the studs and adding the formal bow tie before working on the cuff links he'd had sent up with the other accessories. Then he crossed to the little writing desk in the living area and quickly penned a note for Elizabeth before slipping into new Italian leather shoes and the rest of his tux and letting himself out of the suite.

He had a lot of things to do if he was going to get married tonight.

She knew he was gone when she woke.

Rafe was an overwhelming presence; if he were still in the suite, she would know. She stretched and immediately a thousand small sensations reminded her of his lovemaking. Though there was no one there to see, she smiled a slow, happy smile of contentment. At least physically she was sure that he wanted her.

Slowly she sat up, then rose from the bed and padded into the bathroom. Donning one of the luxurious robes that were compliments of the casino, she used the facilities and washed her face, then went to the mini-bar and got a large bottle of spring water.

On the bar lay a note. The first time she had seen Rafe's handwriting, she'd been privately amused. She could have predicted the bold, aggressive strokes like these in which he explained that he'd had clothing and accessories sent up, that she should go ahead and dress and he'd be back by…oh, heavens!

The clock on the wall told her she had little more than twenty minutes before his return. If she wanted to be beautiful, she'd better get moving. She snatched up the toiletries and cosmetics and headed for the bathroom.

She took the quickest shower on record. As she was slipping into the strappy little sandals that were in one of the boxes, she heard the door of the suite open. Hastily she crossed to the vanity area and picked up her bag, applying a quick dash of lipstick. Then with a nervousness she didn't entirely understand, she started for the door leading to the living room.

Before she could get there, the door opened.

Rafe seemed to fill the doorway, and she was struck by his size, as she always was when she saw him after an absence. His shoulders were so broad, they blocked the light behind him.

"Sleep well?" His voice was warm as he started across the room.

"Yes, I—Rafe!"

He'd seized her by the waist and pulled her up against him. Her protest was purely a formality because already she was winding her arms about his neck and relaxing into his embrace. He put a finger beneath her chin and lifted her face up to his, then cupped her jaw as he set his mouth on hers and parted her lips with his, invading the tender depths with his tongue until she curled against him in restless surrender.

When he lifted his head, he was smiling complacently, a purely male expression of satisfaction. "I'd like to keep you naked in bed for the rest of the evening, but I'd better feed you, for the baby's sake."

She stepped back, smoothing her dress as a warm feeling of hope spread through her. He sounded so tender and concerned...maybe there was a chance he could come to care for her the way she wanted—no, *needed*—him to.

He linked his fingers through hers and held her hands wide. "You look beautiful." Then he grinned. "I've seen pictures of your mother at your age and you're a dead ringer."

She shrugged, smiling. "Strong genes, I guess."

"No wonder your father says he never had a chance." Then his face sobered and his gaze slid down to the gentle curve of her abdomen barely noticeable in the unbelted pale pink dress. "If this baby's a girl, I'm going to have to lock her up to keep the boys away."

Her smile faded as he escorted her out the door and they turned down the hallway to the elevators. "I don't want my child to be as shielded from the world as I was. Until I was ten or so, I thought everyone's parents employed bodyguards around the clock.''

Rafe nodded. ''I can see why your father is so overprotective, though.''

''Yes.'' It was on the tip of her tongue to tell him about Sam Flynn, the man she was going to look up when she got back to Phoenix—the man who might be her brother. She'd been neglecting her duty—it was time to call and see if he had returned to work. She made a private vow to do exactly that first thing in the morning. But instead she said, ''Mother and Father were devastated when James was kidnapped.'' She shuddered and put a hand protectively over her stomach. ''I can't even imagine what it must have been like.''

''No.'' Rafe's face was grim. ''I'm sure losing his only male heir was devastating to your father, especially since he never had another son.''

She glanced up at him, frowning. ''Losing his *child* was devastating to my father.''

''It was a terrible thing,'' he agreed. The elevator bell rang and the doors slid open. ''Shall we go, my pretty princess?''

First they walked out to the front of the hotel, where he secured her a place at the rail in front of the volcano. Despite the warmth, it still got dark relatively early and already the sun was gone. After a short wait, the volcano erupted.

Elizabeth was delighted by the display. Then he hustled her down to Treasure Island just in time to watch the British man-o'-war engage the pirate ship in battle. She clapped when the cannons flashed, and when the British ship finally sank with its captain bravely going down with his command, she gasped at the sight of the lone tricorne floating on the waves. When the ship rose again after a long, tense wait, and the actor portraying the captain spouted a stream of water high into the air, she laughed herself silly.

Next, he took her to a chic French restaurant which boasted burgundy leather seats, quaint low-lit lamps and wildflowers on tables covered in lace-edged linens. After seating her and allowing the maitre d' to unfurl napkins edged in matching lace across their laps, he smiled across the table at her. "It seems a crime to come to a place like this and not drink wine, but you aren't permitted to have alcohol."

"One small glass would be acceptable," she said. "Nutritional value, you know."

He arched an eyebrow. "Umm-hmm. If you say so."

They chatted over dinner, the small, getting-to-know-you rituals that couples on a normal date would enjoy. Because he seemed so fascinated, she let him draw her out, telling him story after story of the scrapes she and her sisters had gotten into as children.

They both declined dessert and while Rafe drank strong coffee and she had a cup of decaffeinated tea, she seized an opening in the conversation to ask him a few questions. It was like pulling teeth with a pair of tweezers, but finally he told her about completing Oxford and deciding to study architecture at Harvard, a move which had appalled his father. Though Rafe didn't elaborate, she sensed there was a great deal more to the story.

"So how did you get from Harvard to owning a Phoenix construction company?"

He shrugged. "I decided I wanted to design unique structures. But I also wanted to see them built to the standards I envisioned, so creating my own company seemed a logical next step."

"This can't have made your father happy." She thought about the Grand Duke she knew. "He's big on tradition.

Doesn't he want you nearby, taking over the reins from him one day?''

A heavy silence fell over the table. ''My father's plans for my life are irrelevant,'' he finally said in a tone that indicated discussion was at an end. ''He threatened to disown me when I wouldn't fall in line, though he hasn't resorted to that yet. Periodically he stops in Phoenix or calls just to browbeat me, thinking I'm going to get less bull-headed as I age. So if your father hoped to cement his relationship with Thortonburg through me, he made a major miscalculation. He'd have done better to throw you at my younger brother.''

The words were such an unexpected attack that she felt as if he'd leaned across the table and struck her. Very slowly, she set down her teacup with trembling hands. ''I've told you before, my father isn't the least interested in arranging marriages for any of his daughters. My parents fell in love and married, and they have given us the same opportunity.''

Rafe snorted. ''My father and your father made an agreement decades ago to marry one of you off to me. I expected it would be the eldest—''

''Alexandra.''

''But for some reason they must have decided you would be more suitable.'' He chuckled, but there was no mirth in the sound. ''Obviously, they had no idea just how well we suit each other or they'd never have left us alone.''

The perfect filet she'd eaten rolled in her stomach at the callous reference to what she had been hoping was love-making. A wave of nausea, so strong that she had to grit her teeth, made her set her napkin aside and reach for her purse. ''I'm going to visit the ladies' and then I'll be ready to leave. I'll meet you in the entry.''

Rafe rose, a frown of concern creasing his broad brow. ''You don't look well.''

"I'm not."

"I knew you shouldn't have had that wine. Is there anything I can do?"

"You've done quite enough, thank you." Her words were clipped and she saw his eyes narrow at the tone, but she was past caring. The beat of her heart in her chest was nearly painful as she pushed away the hopes she'd had of love. Rafe had been hurt in the past, but he wouldn't share that part of himself with her. And she couldn't live with a man who couldn't love her, no matter the reason.

Six

Elizabeth was so quiet on the drive back to the hotel that Rafe could feel his gut twist with worry. She'd started getting weird again when he'd mentioned their fathers and the marriage deal. Mentally he kicked himself. That had upset her before, as well. He should have remembered. What did it matter if she didn't want to believe she was part of an arranged marriage? Women liked a little romance. Well, he thought, she'd forget about their conversation soon enough when she saw what he had done for her.

He led her back to their room and passed his keycard through the lock, then opened the door and motioned for her to precede him. As she did so, he pressed the button on the entry wall for the lamps in the living area.

Halfway into the room, she stopped dead.

Behind her he was grinning. The florist had done a good job. On the glass table in front of the couch stood a huge crystal vase with an arrangement of red roses, three dozen if they'd done as he ordered, beautifully displayed against a background of greenery and some fine-textured, airy white stuff.

"What's this?" Her voice sounded strange.

"They're for you." He stepped forward and took her hand, drawing it to his lips. "For the mother of my child."

She half turned and her eyes were wide as she stared up at him. Then she burst into tears and bolted into the bedroom, sobbing.

What the hell—? He was so stunned, he didn't react at all for a moment.

Then he sprinted to the bedroom door as a feeling of déjà vu assailed him. She wasn't locking him out again!

But the doorknob turned easily beneath his hand. The bedroom was empty and he could hear water running in the adjoining bathroom. Tentatively he knocked on the door. "Elizabeth?"

"Just a moment." Her voice sounded strained and muffled.

She didn't sound as if she planned on camping in there for the night, so he lounged against the closest bureau and waited. It took a while, but finally the doorknob turned and she opened the door. The skin around her eyes was red and puffy, but she wasn't crying, at least.

He straightened. "What's wrong?"

She sighed. "Nothing. Thank you for the roses. They're beautiful." But her tone was lackluster and she looked at the floor rather than at him. "I'm very tired," she said. "I'd like to go to bed."

"All right." He knew perfectly well she meant *alone,* but there wasn't a chance of that. He walked back into the other room and locked the door for the night, then turned off the lights in the living area. By the time he returned, she'd slipped out of the pink dress and wore nothing but the silky undergarments he'd bought her.

She turned, startled, as he came back into the bedroom, but he ignored her reaction, crossing to the bath to turn out the lights. Then he rounded his side of the bed and casually began to undress, removing the tux jacket and unfastening his cuff links and studs.

"What are you doing?" Her voice had the same odd tone it had carried when she'd seen the roses.

Calmly he continued undressing, stepping out of his clothes until he wore nothing but his briefs. "Getting ready for bed. I thought you said you were tired."

"I am." She paused and made a helpless gesture with one hand. "I didn't intend to sleep with you."

"There's only one bed," he pointed out.

"No!" Her voice rose an octave. "I am not sharing a bed with you. Not for sleeping, not for…for any other activity, either."

He'd had it with guessing what was going through her head. Slowly, deliberately, he began to walk around the bed to where she stood.

She took a step backward for every one of his until finally she was literally backed against a wall and he was directly in front of her. If she wanted to get away from him now, she'd have to crawl across the bed.

"I thought you'd like the roses," he said. "I'm sorry if they upset you. Will you please tell me why?"

She hesitated, opened her mouth, closed it again. Finally she said, "Red roses are for lovers, for—for special relationships."

Now he was the one to hesitate. Slowly, feeling as if he was walking down a tunnel without a single glimmer of light, he said, "You…are special to me. Not just because you're going to have my child."

Her eyes were shadowed in the light of the single bedside lamp she'd lit. She shook her head. "Don't sugarcoat it,

Rafe. If I weren't pregnant, if I hadn't come and sought you out, we'd never have seen each other again.''

He opened his mouth automatically to protest. Then he shut it abruptly. She might be right. Five months ago—hell, *one* month ago—he couldn't have imagined himself feeling like this, couldn't have imagined his life without her. She'd been there in the back of his mind for months, and now that she was in his life he wasn't letting her go. Baldly, he said, ''You're probably right. If you'd stayed in Wynborough, we never would have seen each other again. But—'' he reached out and slowly cupped the warm, soft flesh of her cheek in his hand, framing her jawline with his thumb ''—you did come after me. You were smarter than I was. And I'm glad. I don't want to be without you. Not because of the baby. Because of *you*.''

She swallowed. He felt the movement beneath his hand. ''Rafe, I can't—''

''Shhh.'' He stepped closer, gathering her into his embrace, rubbing his chin over the top of her head and tucking her against his heart. ''Don't analyze it to death. Just accept it.''

Bending his head, he kissed her temple then her cheek, then tilted up her face with his thumb beneath her chin and brushed soft kisses over her eyelids, the bridge of her nose, finally nuzzling his way down to her mouth. She was warm and soft and pliant in his arms and he could feel her begin to tremble as she became aware of the arousal he couldn't hide as his body reacted to the scents and feel of woman, *his* woman.

''I want you,'' he said against her mouth. He bent his knees and kissed her throat, then trailed tiny kisses down the smooth flesh swelling at her breasts until the silky fabric of her slip stopped him. ''May I?'' he whispered.

She was leaning back against the wall now, her hands in his hair, eyes closed. Without opening them she nodded her permission, and his blood heated as he realized he'd convinced her to stay with him.

Slowly he reached down and found the hem of the slip, drawing it over her head. Her bra clasped in the front and he set his fingers at the little hook, gently snapping it apart and pushing it back off her shoulders, letting her pretty, pink-tipped breasts bob free. She was so beautiful. His throat grew tight at the realization that she was his now. He wondered if she knew he never planned to let her get away...but this wasn't the time to discuss it. Slowly he raised his hands, cupping the soft, full globes in his palms and gently brushing his thumbs back and forth across the nipples.

She began to breathe faster, her head lolling back against the wall, and the lamplight slanted across her face, making her look mysterious and sensual and desirable. He bent again and placed his mouth right at the place where her breasts met in the center, licking his way down the sweet crevice and then continuing on around the base of one pretty mound. He moved his hand and flicked his tongue over her flesh in an ever-decreasing spiral until finally, he was nearly at the peaked nipple. But he didn't close his mouth over the enticing tip until she moaned and her hands came up to his head, threading through his hair to cradle his skull and guide him to her.

Victorious, he suckled the tight bud, lashing it again and again with his tongue, moving finally to treat the other nipple to the same attentions. Her fingers clenched and loosened and clenched again in his hair, and the unconscious actions fired his own arousal, pushing him heavily against the restraining fabric of his briefs and making him ache with the need to bury himself within her.

But he wanted this time to last. He wanted her to want him, to need the sweet invasion of his body as badly as he needed to immerse himself in her hot depths. And so he lingered over her breasts, suckling strongly then gently laving the puckered flesh until she was quivering before him, her hips shifting in small circles, tiny moans escaping her throat each time he increased the sweet torture.

Finally he allowed her hands to push him down, away from her breasts and he trailed his lips over the satiny flesh of her abdomen to the swell that contained his child. Turning his head, he slid to his knees and lay his cheek against her, savoring the sweetness of the moment. But she was too needy to be satisfied with such gentle actions and soon he explored the tender flesh below with his mouth until the edge of her panties, riding low beneath the fullness of her womb, made him pause.

He grasped the lacy fabric with his teeth and tugged gently, pulling the garment down, burying his nose in the spicy curls that lay exposed before him. Hooking his fingers into the fabric, he slid her panties down and off, and sat back to view the results of his labor.

If he could stand the thought of another man seeing her nude, he'd have her painted just like this, head thrown back, red hair a wild tangle down her back, hands braced on the wall behind her and one leg cocked slightly open, inviting him to search the sweetness hidden in her shadows. But there was no way any other man was getting within a mile of her naked glory. He didn't care how primitive and possessive it sounded. She was his and his alone. Forever.

The thought shook him slightly. And because it was an uncomfortable one to contemplate, he let her siren's call distract him, freeing himself from his confining briefs, letting his straining flesh spring free in anticipation. Leaning forward again, he placed his mouth directly over the shadowed crease in her feminine mound, gently blowing a warm stream of breath over her. She made a low sound of surprise, and he drew back, putting his hands on the insides of her thighs and shifting her stance wide, baring her pink, pouting flesh to his gaze.

His own body was urging him to move faster, but he resisted its pleas. Leaning forward yet again, he used his tongue to open her slick softness and when she cried out, he plunged deeply into her, tasting the hot wet warmth of woman that greeted him. He lifted a hand and rubbed his fingers along the plump folds until he could enter her easily with one finger. As she arched against his hand, he set his mouth over the tiny nubbin that he knew awaited his touch, stroking over it with a rhythmic licking that he mimicked with the movement of his finger.

She was crying with each breath, her hips plunging, her hands in fists beating against the wall. She tolerated only a few of his intimate caresses before she climaxed, her body squeezing his finger in tight, hard contractions as her knees gave way and she began to slide down the wall to the floor.

He would have liked to wait, wanted to spin out the pleasure even more, but he was so hard even the brush of his flesh against his own belly pushed him dangerously close to release. Frantically, he took her by the hips and guided her down onto his jutting staff, arching up and plunging deeply into her just as a series of harsh, hard pulses left him gasping for breath, his head bowed as weakly on her shoulder as hers was on his.

When he could breathe enough to speak again, he chuckled softly. "How in the hell am I going to manage to go six weeks without this after the baby comes?"

She lifted her head from his shoulder and though she still sat astride him, though their bodies were still sweaty and joined together, there was a distant quality to her smile. "You managed for five months last time."

He wanted to shake her. Instead, he leaned forward and nipped lightly at the smooth flesh of her shoulder. "Yes, but that was when I'd convinced myself you were a figment of my imagination."

She yelped and shrank back. "Your imagination?" She sounded slightly indignant.

"My imagination," he repeated. "Too good to be true. A hallucination caused by years of disappointing experiences. I wanted the real thing so badly that I created it. Or so I thought."

"And this is the real thing?"

"I'm going to pretend I didn't hear that," he said, frowning to disguise his smile. Little smart aleck. He took her by the shoulders and pulled her forward, kissed her hard and deep one final time and then lifted her off him.

She promptly collapsed in a heap on the floor.

Groaning as his cramping leg muscles protested, he stood and pulled back the covers on the bed, then lifted her and laid her on the mattress. She immediately snuggled into the pillow, and he patted the smooth, bare buttock she presented before turning out the light and climbing in behind her. He gathered her into his arms and as he closed his eyes and sank into the sweet oblivion of sleep, he felt more content than he could ever remember feeling before in his life.

The morning's bright white light streamed into the room through the sheer curtains over the window, slowly calling him awake. He'd forgotten to close the heavier drapes the night before. It didn't really matter, though. They needed to get up and get going today anyway.

Elizabeth stirred in his arms. Or rather, beneath his arm. During the night she'd stretched out flat on her stomach. He lay on his side with one arm and one leg possessively chaining her to him. He smiled at the thought.

"Good morning, Sleeping Beauty."

"Mmm. G'morning." She turned onto her side, then

rolled onto her back. "What am I going to do when I can't sleep on my stomach anymore?" she asked the ceiling.

"I guess you'll just have to let me hold you all night," he offered.

She turned into his arms, snuggling in and pressing small kisses across his chest. "That sounds nice."

"Elizabeth." He spoke slowly and quietly, not wanting to disturb her unduly. This was going to be the tricky part. Turning his head, he kissed her temple, his thumb caressing the ball of her shoulder where his arm lay around her. "We should get married."

As he'd expected, her body stiffened. She didn't pull away, though, and he was cautiously optimistic. Maybe she'd realized that what they had between them on the physical plane was extraordinary, that some people lived entire lives without experiencing the connection they had.

Finally, she spoke. "I believe we already had this discussion. No, thank you."

"Why not?" His instinct was to lift himself over her and demand that she acquiesce, but he knew her well enough by now to know that that approach would get him nowhere.

"Physical infatuation isn't a good enough foundation for a lifetime together."

"But it's a solid part of that foundation," he argued. "How many married couples do you suppose *aren't* sexually attracted?"

"It's only a part, though, as you just said." There was a hint of sad weariness in her voice. "And it's about the only part we do have."

"We have more than that," he insisted.

"Rafe, I'm not going to marry you and that's final." Her body was stiff and unresponsive, and suddenly he couldn't stand to be in the bed where she'd been so warm and sweet the night before.

Heaving himself upright, he stalked into the bathroom to

shower and shave, then donned the second set of clothes he'd ordered for himself yesterday. While he dressed, he steeled himself to do what he was going to have to do if she continued to be stubborn.

Damn woman! He couldn't understand the wall of resistance she erected each time he mentioned marriage.

Walking back into the bedroom, he said, "I'll ask you one more time. Elizabeth, will you *please* marry me?"

She was looking out the window, clad only in a sheer dressing gown; all he could see was her profile as her lips formed the word, "No."

He sighed. "Then you leave me no choice." He walked across the room and picked up the telephone. Fishing his wallet out of the pants he'd flung across a chair the night before, he extracted a piece of paper and started punching in the numbers.

"What are you doing?"

"Calling your father."

"My father!" She turned her head and glared at him. "Put that telephone down."

He ignored her.

"Why are you calling my father?"

"To tell him that you're pregnant with my child, and you won't marry me even though I've begged you to." He knew it was harsh, but he sensed that there was no other way to force her to agree, and he was determined. His child was going to have his name, and Elizabeth was never leaving him again.

"No!" Her response sounded so agonized that Rafe had to steel himself not to take her in his arms again and comfort her.

Slowly he replaced the receiver and turned to face her. "Why not?"

Elizabeth swallowed. Her gaze was still defiant, but he sensed the decisiveness draining away from her and gradually her defiance changed to a sad acceptance. "I'll marry you," she said quietly. "Just don't tell my parents."

"You're going to have to tell them sometime."

"I know." She shook her head and looked away. "You don't understand. I should be the one to tell them."

"All right." He eyed her. "We'll go get married."

"What? You mean *today?*" She rounded on him and her face went slack with shock for a moment. Then almost as quickly, the fire that he was beginning to recognize lay just beneath the surface of her ladylike demeanor flashed in her eyes. "You had this planned all along," she accused. "Even before I got on that plane yesterday morning, you intended to force me to marry you today. Didn't you? *Didn't you?*" she demanded when he remained silent.

Rafe regarded her for a moment, lightning bolts zinging his way from those emerald eyes. Finally he raised both hands in surrender. "I hadn't decided for sure, but after last night there isn't any reason why we shouldn't get married. I told you I mean my child to be legitimate. I'm prepared to do whatever I have to do to ensure that this baby never has to question his rightful heritage."

She all but sneered. "Noble words for a man who's turned his back on his own heritage."

The barb was a direct hit. "Bull."

"Hah." She crossed her arms and regarded him scornfully. "You're afraid to face your own family. The one time you were near your home in more than a decade, you came incognito and didn't even speak to your parents before sneaking off."

"I'm not afraid of my family," he said, feeling rage welling up from a hidden cache deep in his mind. His lip curled. "They've already done everything they can to make me buckle under and it hasn't worked."

Her face lit with the curiosity he was beginning to realize

was an integral—if damned annoying—part of her personality. "What did they do?"

"Never mind." He knew he sounded like a surly schoolboy, but the memories bombarding him made him feel like a child again as he relived some of the scenes he'd endured with his father.

I never said he wasn't a nice boy. But he's the butcher's son. Hardly a suitable companion for you, Raphael. I've already explained to his family that the friendship simply cannot continue.

With an effort, he shook off the voices from his past, focusing on the woman who would be his future. "Just be dressed and ready to go in thirty minutes."

"I'm having breakfast and taking a shower first," she said. "I'm not going to rush around just so you can be on whatever little schedule you have planned."

"Fine. Will sixty minutes be enough?"

"Plenty. Shall I meet you at the bar?"

He was still trying to forget the things her question had called to mind. "All right. I'll have another dress sent up. Be in the bar in an hour."

"Yes, sir."

He ignored the pert salute she aimed his way as he left the suite and stalked toward the elevator.

Hours later, she remained so angry, she couldn't stand still as she waited impatiently for the royal limo to be called to the VIP queue. As she paced back and forth, she checked her watch. By now, Rafe knew she'd gone and unless he was a lot less resourceful than she suspected, he knew she'd boarded an international flight. And he knew she was going home.

It hadn't been easy. She'd placed one quick call to Laura Bishop at the Colton ranch. Laura had agreed to make her travel arrangements and called back a short time later with all the necessary information.

Laura also agreed to explain to Alexandra that so far Sam Flynn had been unavailable. Elizabeth had hoped so much that she and her sisters would be able to locate the man they were all convinced was their brother, kidnapped as an infant and presumed dead. Only he hadn't been killed, after all. And though the records at The Sunshine Home for Children had left something to be desired, she and her sisters had narrowed down the field of possibilities. Now only two remained: Sam Flynn, the man she had been supposed to make contact with in Phoenix, and John Colton, the younger brother of Alexandra's new husband, Mitch, who, according to Mitch, was unable to be contacted until he decided to show up.

Elizabeth felt bad about letting her sisters down just when they were getting close to finding their brother, but... They would understand, she was sure. She had to talk to her parents before Rafe did. After that, Laura could make sure Sam Flynn was available before Elizabeth returned to speak with him.

With her conscience resting easier, she'd packed rapidly. Then she'd sneaked out of the hotel and caught a flight with minutes left in the hour he'd granted her. At JFK, she'd left her connecting flight to board the private plane her father had sent at Laura's request.

The limo arrived and before she was ready, before she really wanted to be there, she was being driven through the familiar gates of the palace to the main entry stairs where her mother and father, wearing smiles wide enough to crack their faces, waited to greet her. They hurried down the steps as the chauffeur opened the door, and as she slid out, she was enveloped in her mother's arms.

She knew the moment her mother realized what the bulge between them was. Gabriella's body stiffened. She pulled away and stood back, holding Elizabeth at arm's length to look at her. *All* of her. Shock, surprise, bewilderment all flashed across the Queen's face. Then compassion filled her eyes.

"Oh, my darling," she said. "Is this an occasion for celebration? Are you happy about this?"

"Happy about what?" Her father's voice boomed over her mother's softer tones.

"Brace yourself, Phillip," said Queen Gabriella. "Our little girl is pregnant." She shepherded Elizabeth up the steps as she spoke, issuing orders to the staff for refreshments in the family drawing room.

"Pregnant! But where...who...how...?" The King's voice trailed off into astonished silence as he strode along at his wife's heels.

"I imagine we'll learn *where* the father is and *who* the father is very shortly, dear," her mother said over her shoulder. "And if you don't know *how* by now, I truly despair of you."

Despite the tears that threatened to fall, Elizabeth had to giggle. She'd been so afraid to tell them. Well, afraid wasn't exactly the right word. More like sorry. She knew being an unwed mother must be the last thing her parents wanted for one of their daughters. She'd put off this moment for so long because she hadn't been able to face the thought of their disappointment in her.

And there was another reason, as well.

They *had* to locate James! If they didn't, and if this baby she carried was a son...she couldn't bear to think about what it would mean for her child. Please, God, let this be a girl.

"So." Her mother pressed her into a wingbacked chair and lifted her feet onto the matching hassock, making Elizabeth smile. "Would you like something to drink?"

"Some kind of juice would be wonderful. Cranberry, please?"

Her mother nodded, and the hovering maid took off at light speed. Anyone in the palace employ who hadn't already heard that Princess Elizabeth had come home with a baby on the way would know in a matter of minutes, she was sure.

One more reason she dreaded the idea of raising her child in the palace environment in which she'd been raised.

"How are you feeling?" her mother asked.

Simultaneously the king asked, "Do you know if it's a boy?"

Her father was pacing back and forth in front of the wide windows, looking rather...agitated. She supposed he had the right to be.

"I feel fine," she answered her mother. "A little bit of morning sickness early on, but now I couldn't feel better." Unbidden, an image of the heated lovemaking she had experienced only hours ago flashed through her head and she felt herself blush.

Her mother raised her eyebrows with a knowing smile, but didn't comment.

"I'm about five months along," Elizabeth went on. "The baby's due in mid-June. And, no, I don't know its gender. We'll have to wait and be surprised."

"Is the father in the picture?" Her own father had stopped his pacing and turned to toss the question at her.

Elizabeth hesitated. "Yes. But not in the way you might hope."

"In other words, he's not prepared to marry you." Her father was glowering.

"No, Daddy," she said, smiling gently. "It's the other way around. *I'm* the one who won't marry *him.*"

"Does this man have a name you'd like to share with

us?'' her mother asked. "If you'd rather not, I suppose we can accept that.''

Elizabeth couldn't think of anything she wanted to do less, but she knew there was no point in hiding it. The truth would come out sooner or later. Sooner probably, if she knew Rafe. She wasn't stupid enough to think that this was anything but a successful skirmish in what looked to be a long siege.

"He has a name," she said reluctantly. "You know him.''

"The Prince of Thortonburg," her father said.

"Yes. Although he goes by Rafe Thorton these days.'' She looked at him in surprise. "Has he already spoken to you?''

"No, but it makes sense," her father said. "That young man couldn't shake his royal title fast enough to suit him. When he told me you'd be staying with him, it seemed out of character.''

"Raphael.'' Her mother smiled. "I always did like his spirit. Victor never succeeded in training that one to his ridiculously outdated notions of aristocratic conduct.''

"He didn't know who I was when we...when we... met.'' Her face felt hot again, and the disappointment in her mother's eye didn't help.

"I see,'' the Queen said.

"He was upset at first," Elizabeth confessed. "As you said, he doesn't have a very high opinion of royalty. But once he'd gotten over the shock, he decided we would get married.''

"And that's a problem for you?'' her mother asked in a soft voice. She stood and came around behind the chair, setting her hands on Elizabeth's shoulders and rubbing gently.

"I don't want to be married out of duty.''

"Is that the only reason he wants to marry you?''

Elizabeth shrugged and avoided the question. "This is all Serena's fault. She's the one who talked me into tracking him down and telling him."

Her father turned from the window. "Coming from Serena, that was amazingly sensible." But his voice was indulgent and he was smiling. Serena had been a handful since the day she was born. Every silver hair in his head could be attributed to her, he'd said more than once.

"Daddy..." She hesitated, feeling ridiculous for even asking the question when she knew the answer. Still... "Rafe has some notion that you and his father arranged, or at least promised, that he'd marry one of us. I told him it's not true." But she knew her eyes were asking her father for the truth.

Phillip shook his head. "Victor hounded me about that for years. I always told him that I'd never oppose a match if one of my daughters chose either of his sons. As you said, it's not true." The King hesitated. "Does Thortonburg understand the manner in which the Wynborough crown is passed on?"

Elizabeth shook her head. "I—I'm not sure."

Her mother clucked her tongue. "You'd better be sure, dear. If this child is the first-born grandson to the King—"

"I know." Elizabeth linked her fingers. "I know."

The King moved to the side of Elizabeth's chair and bent to press a kiss to her cheek. "I have an appointment with the Minister of Public Works, but when I return I want to be filled in completely."

As he rose, a commotion in the hallway had them all turning. Trained to react instantly to threatening situations, the guard on duty slammed the door shut. As he did so, Elizabeth could see him drawing the gun from his holster.

Then she recognized the voice echoing down the hall, though it had an imperious quality that she'd never associated with it before. "...Thortonburg and I'm going to be marrying the Princess Elizabeth, so *do not* tell me they're unavailable. I'll search every damned room of this palace if I have to."

She half rose from her chair, but the King moved faster. Throwing open the door to the room, he spoke at the top of his considerable voice. "The Prince of Thortonburg is welcome. Put away your arms, everyone. Thank you for your vigilance, though in this instance it isn't necessary."

Elizabeth closed her eyes. If Rafe had wanted a demonstration of the ridiculous lengths her father went to with security, she couldn't have provided a better one if he'd specifically asked.

When she opened her eyes again, he was there, striding into the room. Bigger, as always, than she remembered and looking as totally furious as she'd ever seen him. His expression today made his face the day he'd found her by her broken-down rental car look almost friendly.

His blue eyes speared her in the chair where she sat, and he took three steps forward before realizing he was in the presence of the King. Abruptly, he spun and bowed formally from the waist. "Your Majesty."

He crossed to the Queen and took the hand she extended, bowing low over it and kissing it in a formal salutation. "Your Majesty."

"Welcome, Raphael."

Before the Queen could add anything else, Rafe stalked around to stand before Elizabeth. He held out his hand in regal demand, and when she placed hers in it, he bowed again. But he didn't give her hand the perfunctory peck she expected. Instead, he turned it over and slowly, leisurely pressed a kiss into the center of her palm. When she felt his tongue tracing secret patterns on her flesh, she tried to jerk her hand away, but Rafe held it firmly for another moment before raising his head. "Your Royal Highness."

"Subservience doesn't suit you," Elizabeth said, snatching her hand back and linking it tightly with the other in her lap, ignoring both her mother's snort of amusement and the leap of her own pulse at his touch. "So just stop it. How on earth did you get here so fast?"

"Ever heard of private planes?" His voice was surly. Grouchy. Thoroughly out of sorts. She guessed she couldn't blame him.

"Raphael, Elizabeth has just finished telling us of your intentions." King Phillip stepped forward. Gone was the indulgent father, and in his place was the commanding monarch few ever saw in action.

"Good." Rafe didn't even appear to notice the monarch's attitude. "Then you know that I have chased your stubborn, spoiled, opinionated daughter across the Atlantic Ocean because I intend to marry her. I shouldn't think that would be a problem for you."

"Of course not." The King's stern face softened slightly. "You are more than welcome in this family…*if* you can convince my 'stubborn, spoiled, opinionated daughter' to marry you." He looked over Elizabeth's head to his wife, then, offering her his arm, said, "Come, my dear. These young people have things to discuss."

"Really, that's not necessary," Elizabeth began, turning around, trying to send her mother a silent message with her eyes. "Mother, you don't have to leave."

"I'm afraid duty calls me, as well," the Queen said, shrugging as if she were helpless to alter the matter. She winked at Elizabeth—winked!—and took her husband's arm as the two of them exited the room.

Seven

A heavy silence fell. She kept her eyes on her clasped hands, refusing to look at Rafe. Finally, when he didn't speak, she could stand the suspense no longer. "You can't make me marry you."

"All right."

She raised her head abruptly and stared at him. "All right?"

He shrugged, and the motion of his wide shoulders shifted the fabric of the fine leather jacket he wore. "I can't force you to marry me. We'll let a judge decide what kind of custody arrangements would work best."

"You—you wouldn't do that." She put a hand to her throat.

"By now you should know me well enough to realize I mean exactly what I say."

"But that's half the problem," she said heatedly. In her agitation she rose from the chair and gestured wildly with her hands. "I *don't* know you. We've spent a total of only a few weeks in each other's company in our entire lives. How can you think we could make a marriage work?"

Standing had been a mistake. Rafe stepped toward her, slipping his arms around her and gently rubbing his big hands up and down her spine. "Why couldn't we? Lots of people make successful marriages from much less." His embrace felt so wonderful, his arms so strong and secure, that she could feel her willpower draining away like an overused battery.

"Name some." Her voice was muffled against his chest.

"That's easy. My parents."

She looked up at him. Another mistake. His hard lips and the enticing dimples grooving his cheeks were much, much too close. Hastily she put a hand against his chest, holding him away when he would have pulled her closer. "No kissing!" She could see the amusement gleaming in his eyes. Averting her gaze, she stared at the metal zipper tab where he'd left it halfway up its track on his jacket. "Was their marriage arranged?"

"Their families wanted to cement a business relationship," Rafe said. "My grandfather ran through enough of the Thortonburg money that a marriage to a wealthy noblewoman was a necessity for my father."

"How sad." She couldn't imagine having her husband picked out for her. "My father did the exact opposite. He defied his own father to marry a penniless American. Quite a scandal at the time." She smiled. "But they never have regretted it."

"They seem very happy." Rafe sounded almost as if he doubted it. "But we aren't discussing your parents. We're talking about us. When I realized you'd slipped out of Vegas without me—"

A knock at the door interrupted whatever he had been going to say. Hastily, Elizabeth pulled herself away from his embrace and smoothed her wrinkled travel clothes. "Come in."

"Welcome home, Your Highness." The tall, handsome man in the uniform of royal security stopped before her and bowed over Elizabeth's hand.

"Lance!" Ignoring protocol, Elizabeth reached up to hug the dark-haired man. "Lose any princesses lately?"

The guard bared his teeth at her, but his eyes were a warm, smoky gray. "Serena was sly, I'll grant you that. But I will never lose anyone on my watch again. Cost me a promotion, you know."

She laughed. "I hardly think so. I've heard of your recent success." Belatedly she realized Rafe was glaring at the stranger who still had a muscled arm familiarly about her shoulders. "Rafe, this is Lance Grayson—newly appointed head of the Investigative Division of the Royal Security Detail of Wynborough. Recently he had the misfortune to be assigned as my sister Serena's bodyguard." She slipped from beneath Lance's arm and stepped a pace away, aware of the aura of leashed aggression flowing from Rafe. "Lance, may I present the prince of Thortonburg."

There was a silence that lasted a beat too long as the two men, so alike in height and build, assessed each other.

"My Lord Thortonburg." Lance bowed formally.

"When will you be leaving us?" Elizabeth asked.

"This is my final week in the King's employ," Lance informed her.

"Was there a reason for your interruption?" Rafe's tone was courteous, but he left no doubt that he wasn't pleased.

"The King asked me to extend his invitation to stay here at the palace during your visit. If you wish to do so, I'll attend to your personal security."

"Please thank the King for me, but I'll decline his invitation. I've already made arrangements at the Royal Drake Hotel."

"Very good, sir." Lance bowed, turned to Elizabeth and smiled. "I beg your pardon for the intrusion."

As the door closed behind him, Elizabeth rounded on Rafe. "Why were you so rude to Lance?"

"I didn't like how familiar he was with you."

"Don't be ridiculous."

"I'm not." It was nearly a snarl.

Taken aback, she decided it was time for a little soothing of the savage beast. Warily she said, "You're more than welcome to stay here if you like. I'm sure my parents would be pleased."

Rafe gave a bark of laughter that wasn't amused. "Right. Until they caught me sneaking out of your bedroom, you mean." He reached for her so swiftly that she didn't have a chance to evade his arms. "I don't intend to sleep under the same roof with you unless you're in my bed. And I don't intend to sleep under another roof from you for very damn long. You're marrying me. Soon. Before I actually have to kill the next man who puts his hands on you."

His words sent a thrill of purely primitive reaction down her spine, though she refused to admit that his attitude made her feel cherished and protected and...safe. "I didn't say I'd marry you. As I recall, before we were interrupted, we were discussing the possibility of a marriage."

"The eventuality of our marriage."

"The *possibility*," she reiterated.

"There's no good reason we shouldn't marry," Rafe said, pulling her to him again. "Kiss me, Princess. I've been away from you for more than half a day, and now I'm condemned to spend the night elsewhere, too."

"I don't *want* to kiss you," she said irritably. "All that does is confuse the issue." But as his hands roamed down her back and over her bottom, pulling her up against him, she moaned.

"Just think what we could be doing right now if we were

still in Las Vegas.'' His voice was a rough growl in her ear, his breath hot against her cheek. He pushed his hips firmly against her and when she shifted her legs incrementally to give his growing erection a snug home in the warm cove of her thighs, he caught his breath in a harsh gasp. ''You love to tease me, don't you?'' He bent his head and seized her earlobe in his teeth, worrying the sensitive shell with a not-entirely-gentle series of nips.

The stinging sensations, soothed as they were by his agile tongue, were a stimulating caress, and she could feel her breath growing short, her body softening as it set up an insistent throbbing in the one place that so desperately needed his touch. She squirmed against him, rubbing her aching mound against the rigid flesh pushing at her.

''We can't do this here,'' she whispered into his shoulder.

''I know, but isn't it fun pretending for a few minutes?'' His mouth slid down the side of her neck.

She shuddered, feeling her willpower draining away. How could this one man make her brain cells go on holiday every time he touched her? ''Would you really try to take the baby away from me?'' It was an effort to focus.

He stilled against her. Finally his broad chest rose and fell in a heavy sigh. Setting her on her feet away from him, he said, ''I will do anything I have to to get you to marry me, Princess. You're never going to be on the other side of the Atlantic from me again.''

And as she stood there, bereft of his big, warm presence, dazed and trying to comprehend his words, Rafe made an impatient gesture. ''Elizabeth, I want you. Not just today but for a long, long time.'' He didn't sound that thrilled by the admission. ''Can you tell me you don't want me, too?''

She hesitated, but honesty won out. ''No,'' she whispered.

''Then marry me.'' That quickly, she was in his arms

again and he was kissing her with wild, unrestrained passion, his hands roving familiarly over her body, pulling up her sweater to slide his palms around the pliant mounds of her breasts, murmuring in quiet satisfaction. When she dropped her hands to his waist and slid them around him, pulling his lower body against her so that she could feel the proof of his need for her hard and ready against her belly, he growled. Lifting his mouth so that it hovered just above hers, he dropped small, harsh kisses on her lips. *"Marry me."*

"I—" She sighed. "All right."

His big body stilled completely for a moment. Then he kissed her again, only this time there was a tenderness in it that made her heart expand with hope. "You won't be sorry," he promised.

The next day, they made the short flight to Thortonburg and Rafe took her to the vault at Thortonburg Castle where his family's heirloom rings were kept. His family fortune was easily as extensive as Elizabeth's own, and the array of rings he brought out to show her was dazzling even to a woman used to the finest of gems. When she threw up her hands helplessly and told him there were too many beautiful rings to choose from, he leaned forward and picked up a square-cut emerald surrounded by diamonds.

It was a beautiful ring and when he slipped it on her ring finger, it fit as if it had been made for her. "It's a sign," he said in satisfaction. "This ring belonged to my great-great-grandmother on my mother's side. She had green eyes just like you and her husband gave her an entire set of emerald jewelry to match this." He leaned forward and kissed her, lingering over her mouth until they were both panting. "If you're good, I'll give you the rest for a wedding present."

"And just what does 'being good' entail?" She could

hardly believe that throaty purr had come from her own throat.

He chuckled as he rose and rang the bell for the waiting servants to enter and replace the rest of the gems in the vault. "Not nearly enough while we're each sleeping under a different roof," he said "Not *nearly* enough."

He was looking forward to seeing his parents again as much as he looked forward to his biannual dental checkups. And the woman sitting in the passenger seat on his left wasn't going to help the situation any, he thought darkly as he drove the imported luxury car from the royal airstrip through the countryside toward the hills of Thortonburg proper, where his entire family awaited his visit.

They were having dinner with the Grand Duke and Duchess. Elizabeth had been hesitant to accept when his mother Sara had called yesterday with the invitation, and he appreciated her concern for his feelings. Still, he'd told her, it was an excellent way for her to get to know him better, a lure he knew she'd swallow like a trout.

"Tell me more about your childhood." Elizabeth shifted in her seat, and he took his eyes off the road long enough to appreciate the way her skirt climbed up one long, slender thigh. They'd brought evening dress for tonight's dinner, but the simple houndstooth suit with gray suede trim at the collar and cuffs was almost elegant enough to suffice.

Last night, he'd been amazingly miserable without her, considering that they'd only spent one whole night together in the same bed in this whole crazy relationship. And as much as he longed to have her moving under him in ecstasy and sleeping in his arms, he knew there was more to it than that. The days they'd spent together in Phoenix had gotten him accustomed to her presence, to her quiet humming as she flitted around the house, to the gentle scents of perfume—and Elizabeth—that occasionally wafted down the halls. He hadn't particularly wanted to analyze the feeling that had swept over him when he'd presented himself at the palace for luncheon earlier today and seen her come sedately down the hall to greet him.

No, he'd much rather relive the passionate moment they'd shared when he pulled her into the deserted library for a few kisses to tide him over.

"Rafe? Where are you?"

He came back to the present with a jolt. She was eyeing him with what looked to be compassion and he realized she thought he'd been thinking of his childhood.

"My childhood? Not much to say, as I already told you. I was away at school."

"What did you do on holiday?"

A ball of ice formed in his stomach. "I spent most of my holidays at school."

There was a moment of silence as she digested that. But he knew she wouldn't let it go. "Why didn't you go home?"

Raphael! Come down from there at once. Climbing trees is for peasants. Time for your riding lesson and I'll be most unhappy if you're late again.

He shrugged. "I don't know. My father and I didn't get along very well. It seemed…simpler."

Second place in the national geography competition. Second place? *Really, Raphael, we expected more from you than this. The Thorton name is one of the oldest and finest in all Europe…*

"How about your mother?"

"What about her?"

She sighed as if she were dealing with an intransigent child. "Did you get along with your mother?"

"Sure. But when there were any decisions to make, she deferred to Father's judgment."

"How long has it been since you've seen them?"

He counted. "Almost two years. They stopped to harass me briefly on a trip to California."

"Two years! And you haven't been to see them since?" She was truly shocked. He could feel it flowing across the car toward him like a tangible presence. "But..." she was clearly at a loss "...they're your *family*."

"Look," he said, wishing he were anywhere else but having this conversation. "Your parents adore you. Not everyone in the world has the same good fortune. Don't expect them to fall all over themselves with joy at the sight of me." He couldn't suppress the bitter laugh that escaped. "On the other hand, you and I both will probably be honored guests now that my father's gotten what he wants. That baby is his fondest dream."

"Don't tell me we're back to this arranged marriage nonsense. My father says it's not true." Her tone was aggressive, and for the first time a kernel of doubt worked its way into his mind. Was it possible the old goat had lied to him all these years?

But all he said was, "You'll see what I mean."

He turned into the high, gated entrance to the castle a few minutes later. The guard on duty greeted him by his title—his *former* title, he thought grimly as he made the drive through the forested grounds and out through the expanse of lawn to the circular drive that fronted the enormous old keep.

He hoped his father didn't think this visit was made for the purpose of effecting a reconciliation, because nothing could be farther from the truth. The castle might be an outstanding example of Norman architecture, but Roland could have the moldy old ruin—and all the others—as well as the yoke of responsibility that went with them.

As they walked up the wide marble steps of the castle, memories battered at his brain. He'd come up these steps many times as a child. His father would be standing at the top, waiting, and the little boy he'd been dreaded those first words.

Fell from your horse in the polo match. Fell from your horse! If you want the King of Wynborough to consider you a suitable match for one of his daughters, you'll have to do better than that.

The little boy in his memories nodded docilely, but behind the blank face resentment brewed.

"You look positively ferocious." Elizabeth laid a small hand on his arm. "What on earth are you thinking?"

With an effort, he shook off the past. "Just reliving the happy scenes of my youth. Come on, let's get this over with."

But she didn't move forward with him and he stopped and looked at her. "Uh-oh. You don't think we know each other that well, but I already know exactly what you're going to say next."

"You do not." But her voice was indulgent.

"What scenes from your childhood were you reliving?" He did his best imitation of a cracked feminine voice, and she laughed.

"All right. I confess. Maybe it's just that women in general are invariably nosy? And I'm just like every other woman."

"Not a chance." Rafe took her hand and pulled her nearer. "Believe me, there's no other woman on earth like you." He raised her hand to his lips. "And I mean that in the best possible way."

She swallowed, and the rosy blush he so loved warmed her cheeks. He hadn't thought a simple compliment, if it even qualified as such, could unsettle her like that.

"Thank you," she said. But as the heavy door began to swing open, she smiled at him, flashing the little dimple in her cheek he found so fetching. "Don't think you've sidetracked me. We'll get back to this conversation later."

A butler in formal dress opened the door and Rafe noted it was the same stodgy old coot his father had employed for eons.

"Good afternoon, Trumble. How have you been?"

"Very good, my lord. Welcome home." The old man's face was a study in blank disapproval, a look he'd worn since the days when Rafe was a young boy trying to sneak in the kitchen door with the garden snake he'd captured. "May I take your wraps?"

Rafe stepped behind Elizabeth and removed the car coat draped over her shoulders, then handed over his leather jacket. "We have bags in the car. Could you have them taken to a guest suite, please?"

"Certainly, my lord. If you'll follow me…?" As the man turned and started down the hallway, Rafe spoke again.

"Don't bother showing us in, Trumble. I know the way. Family in the drawing room?"

"As you wish, sir." The aged servant nodded stiffly, and Rafe could see his insistence on informality was a source of irritation. Some things never changed. As they moved down the hall, Rafe leaned close to Elizabeth's ear. "Trumble's been here since the place was built. He was born that age and he wins yearly awards for his personality and charm."

She laughed, a soft, musical sound. "He certainly seems a bit on the…sour side."

"Lemons are sugar in comparison, believe me."

They continued down the hall and turned left, heading for the room where he knew the family would be gathered, having their pre-dinner drink. Routine rarely, if ever, varied in his father's house. As they passed a large linen closet, Rafe paused and opened the door. Ha! Empty. Grabbing Elizabeth's wrist, he dragged her behind him into the small, dark room, reaching out to flip on the single light.

She turned her face up to his and her green eyes were wide and alarmed. "What are we doing in here?"

He looked down at her and smiled. Then his gaze dropped to her lips, the luscious field of soft pink slightly parted as she waited for his response. He could see the instant the intimacy of their position dawned on her. Slipping one arm around her, he drew her close while with his other hand he covered her hard little tummy, his fingers nearly brushing the top of the warm feminine mound below as he cupped the small bulge. He slipped one hand up to the back of her neck, drawing her up on tiptoe against him while he still held his other hand over her unborn baby. "Stop thinking so much," he growled as he bent to her lips. "Turn off your brain and go with your instincts."

Then he kissed her, and just as it had every other time he touched her, the world fell away and all he could feel, all he could smell and taste and touch was her, surrounding his senses so that he could think of nothing else. But this time there was a new element of intimacy in the meeting of their mouths, a recognition that this was meant to be. It was as if each of them had realized in their one day apart just how much they needed each other.

"You have to marry me soon," he said, and his voice was so rough and deep and hoarse that it didn't sound like his at all.

There was a moment when her gaze flew up to meet his and he couldn't read her thoughts. A cold arrow of fear shot through him at the idea that he'd been mistaken, that she hadn't really agreed—

"All right."

He might not have heard it if he hadn't been watching her face. Jubilation expanded within him until he thought he might have to shout aloud. But instead he forced himself to release her, then gently turned her around while he brushed the wrinkles out of her skirt and she fished a tissue out of her purse for him to wipe her lipstick from his lips.

"Let's get this over with," he said. "The sooner we can get home to Phoenix, the better."

It was a little like facing a firing squad, she thought, as Rafe opened the double doors. She'd met every one of the three people in the room many times before. *But you weren't pregnant and unmarried,* said the little voice inside her head that still shamed her from time to time.

The Thorton family stood as she preceded Rafe into the room. Though not a one remarked on her pregnant state, she knew it was obvious in the simple wool maternity suit she'd worn, and she felt her cheeks heat in embarrassment at the slight widening of their eyes before they all hastily dragged their gazes to her face.

Training kicked in and she went from one to another, exchanging a small word with each person as Rafe followed behind her. As they approached his father, she caught a flash of deep emotion in the older man's gaze as he looked at his eldest son. But in an instant it was gone, and, after greeting her, the Grand Duke turned to Rafe with a stern cordiality so remote he could have been addressing a peer whom he barely knew.

"Welcome home, Raphael."

"Thank you, Father."

Rafe didn't bother to add any small talk to ease them past the moment, and when she glanced at him, the muscle working in his jaw warned her just how difficult this was for him. Quickly she stepped into the breach.

"My father says you've got an exceptional colt out of the mare you bred to his stallion," she said. Then she blushed as she realized breeding practices probably weren't the wisest topic of conversation under the circumstances.

But Victor Thorton only nodded and smiled at her. "Yes,

indeed. The last time we bred them, we got that pretty little filly who has gone on to win every two-year-old race out there. Your father kept that one, and I'm hoping this colt will be as superb a piece of horseflesh.''

They moved past him then to where the Grand Duchess of Thortonburg stood beside the wingback chair in which she'd been sitting doing needlework before they arrived.

''Your Grace.'' Elizabeth touched her cheek to the older woman's, noting the still-beautiful skin and, more importantly, the open warmth in her green eyes as she gazed at her son. ''Thank you for receiving me.''

''It's my pleasure, dear.'' The Grand Duchess spoke to Elizabeth, but her hungry eyes barely left her son. As Elizabeth moved aside, the slender woman stretched up to enfold her eldest child in her arms. ''Oh, Raphael, it's good to have you home. You've been missed.''

''It's only a visit, Mother.'' Again, Rafe was stiff and abrupt, though Elizabeth noticed his arms tightened for a long moment about his mother's slender frame.

''One we hope you'll repeat often.'' The Grand Duchess smiled serenely, but Elizabeth saw the hurt she couldn't hide.

''And Roland.'' Elizabeth held out both hands to the waiting man. A year younger than she, they'd attended balls and house parties and all manner of things with the same crowd of young aristocrats.

''Princess Elizabeth. It's been too long.'' Roland drew her close and kissed both cheeks.

''Hmm.'' Elizabeth drew back and considered. ''Nearly four months. The last time I saw you, you'd been unseated during a hunt and landed in a mudhole as I recall.''

Roland gave her a mock-scowl, then grinned and her heart stuttered at the resemblance to his brother. ''You have a good memory. Too good.'' He turned to his older brother with his hand extended. ''Welcome home, Raphael.''

"Thank you." Rafe took the outstretched hand and the brothers shook.

An awkward silence fell. It was as if these people didn't know how to make small talk with each other, she thought. Then she realized that was probably the literal truth. Rafe had lived at schools most of his life. Any attempt at "catch-up" conversations would be severely limited because they simply didn't know each other well. Comparing them to her own boisterous, warm, loving family, she felt her heart constrict. No wonder Rafe had trouble allowing himself to feel.

As the silence grew oppressive, she opened her mouth to say something, anything, but Rafe forestalled her by taking her hand in his and holding up the engagement ring he'd given her.

In a curiously formal tone, he said, "Father, Mother, Roland, we have an announcement to make." He paused for a moment and looked down at her, holding her gaze with his as he said, "Elizabeth has agreed to do me the honor of becoming my wife. We'll be married in Wynborough in two weeks."

Two weeks? Suddenly time seemed to be rushing past.

He must have read the shock in her eyes because he smiled then, a small, private smile just for her before turning back to his family. "In case you hadn't noticed, there's a bit of a need for haste," he added wryly.

She was blushing, she knew she was and she made a face at him. Darn the man for pointing out something that didn't need any additional notice.

"Well!" The Grand Duke's tone was too loud, too enthusiastic. "That's wonderful news, Raphael. Congratulations to you both."

The Grand Duchess looked happy but hesitant. "I wasn't aware that you two had ever met," she said.

"We became acquainted at the Children's Fund Ball last

fall,'' Rafe informed her. ''Elizabeth has been a guest in my home in Phoenix recently. We'll be living there after the wedding.''

She had to admire the way he left out all sorts of pesky details which would have required a rather more in-depth explanation.

''But you weren't home at that time—'' Sara Thorton stopped abruptly as she realized that her eldest son had indisputably been in Europe at that time. He simply hadn't chosen to visit his family.

The Grand Duchess bit her lip and turned away, and Elizabeth saw the sheen of tears in the older woman's eyes. ''It was a very quick trip,'' she offered impulsively.

A muffled choking sound from across the room drew her attention. Roland's eyes were dancing with laughter and she realized she was only making things worse. Rafe obviously had had time for *some* things. She could feel her cheeks heating again.

''We'll be married in Wynborough, but we will continue to make our home in Phoenix,'' Rafe said.

''In Phoenix! But you can't take the potential heir to the throne out of the country,'' the Grand Duke protested.

''Elizabeth cannot take the throne,'' Rafe said sharply. ''Alexandra's the eldest, so her firstborn son will ascend the throne. I *do* remember a few things from my classes in governmental policy, Father.''

''There's been a change—''

Rafe's mother cut off her husband's blustering tone. ''Where will the wedding take place?''

''At Wynton Chapel,'' Elizabeth volunteered gratefully. She could practically see Rafe's temper rising perilously close to the boiling point, and apparently his mother did, too. She put a gentle hand on his arm. This topic was *not* one she wanted to discuss at the moment.

The Duchess was determined to get the conversation

back onto safer topics. "Then we'd better get on with the arrangements. I shall call the Queen tomorrow and offer my assistance."

"Thank you, Mother." Rafe stepped forward and kissed her cheek and again Elizabeth saw the woman blink back tears. "Now if you'll excuse us, I'm sure Elizabeth would like to rest before dinner. Is there a room prepared?"

Roland strolled to the door. "Can you imagine that there isn't?"

That succeeded in drawing a chuckle from Rafe and Roland beckoned for them to precede him. "I'll show you to her room."

They followed the younger man to the second level of the old castle and down several long hallways until he halted and turned the knob of a door. Along the way, she surreptitiously watched Rafe's face as he absorbed the ambience of his childhood, but his expression was completely blank and she had no clue as to what was going through his mind. The only suggestion of tension came from the rigid set of his shoulders and the muscle ticking in his jaw.

At the door of the room they all paused. "It really is good to see you again, Roland," she said, breaking the silence that hung between the brothers.

"And you," he responded, reaching for her hand and holding it for just a moment. "Good luck with this baby. It'll be easier if it's a girl, I'm sure. No decisions to be made."

She nodded, and she knew her voice sounded troubled when she answered him. "Thank you."

"Rafe…" The younger man hesitated. "I know it hasn't been easy to come back."

"I wouldn't have come at all if a certain skittish woman hadn't made me chase her through three time zones." Rafe reached out and gave a lock of Elizabeth's hair a gentle tug.

"I know." Roland smiled. "But maybe it's a good thing. You and Father needed this." Then he hesitated. "He's sorry, you know, even if he can't say it. He's been different lately—mellower—largely because it broke his heart to realize he had driven you away."

"You're trying to tell me he learned from his mistakes?" There was sarcasm in Rafe's voice.

The affable mask over Roland's handsome face dropped away, and suddenly Elizabeth felt the aggression that charged the air. The two men faced each other, and if the atmosphere hadn't been so tense, she would have laughed at the sight of the brothers who looked enough alike to be twins but for their age disparity glaring at each other.

"I'm not *trying* to tell you, I *am* telling you," Roland said levelly. "I remember very little of what happened when you two got together. If you can't forgive him, I'll try to understand. But I hope you'll think about it."

Rafe sighed. "You ask a lot."

Roland shrugged, smiling, then he extended his hand. "Thank you for coming, whatever the reason. I'm glad you're here."

Rafe hesitated. Then, grabbing his brother's hand, he pulled the younger man into an awkward embrace. "It surprises me to admit that I'm glad I'm here, too. Thanks."

In the next moment, the door closed behind Roland, and Rafe and Elizabeth were alone in the room. For an instant, he wondered about his brother's odd words when he'd spoken to Elizabeth. But when he looked across the room at his woman, everything else faded from his mind except the need to reassert his claim.

He closed the space between them in three quick steps, taking her by the shoulders and dragging her into his arms.

Eight

"**R**afe!" She squeaked and struggled, but he caught both wrists in one big hand behind her back, arching her against him and rubbing his body back and forth against hers, feeling the heady rush of arousal course through him. Her body was soft and warm and when he bent his head and covered her mouth, she didn't fight him but opened to his probing tongue as if she'd been waiting for him.

Maybe she had. He hoped he wasn't the only one who'd been driven crazy by the hours and the night they'd spent apart.

Lifting his head a fraction, he said, "Do you know how I felt when I realized you were gone?"

Her body stilled. "Furious?" she ventured.

"Well, that, too." He framed her jaw with one big hand. "I was worried sick. Not that you had decided to travel independently—" He forestalled her when she would have spoken again. "You're pregnant. You shouldn't be running around the globe.'' He paused for a moment, and his next words were more of a thought spoken aloud. ''I don't want you away from me overnight ever again.''

Her eyes widened. They stared at each other for a moment and again he recognized that something had changed between them. But her body was calling to him, soft and enticing against him, and he couldn't think of anything but making her his again in the most basic way there was, telling her without words how much she meant to him.

Putting a hand on her hip, he explored the inside of her mouth as he urged her toward the high, antique bedstead with its tapestry canopy. When the backs of her knees bumped against the mattress, he slid his free hand around to palm one smooth, rounded buttock, but the fabric of her skirt got in the way.

Releasing her wrists, he muttered against her mouth, ''Get these clothes off,'' as he plunged his hands beneath her skirt and tugged both her knickers and her tights down and off. She was unbuttoning the line of tiny buttons running down the front of her blouse when he stood again. Impatiently he pulled the blouse and her slip over her head in one smooth move, then tossed them aside and reached for her bra. As he unclasped the garment and drew it aside, her breasts fell free. He cupped them in his palms, feeling their cool weight warming beneath his touch as he slipped his hands around and around in small circles, brushing repeatedly over the sensitive nipples that rose to meet his stroking.

He leaned down and kissed her again, then dropped his head to her shoulder and pressed a kiss to the fine-grained flesh he found there, marveling at the bounty of feminine beauty he'd exposed. She was making small noises in the back of her throat and she brought her hands up between them to deal with the buttons of his shirt, shoving it aside and dragging up his T-shirt beneath to expose his broad, rough-haired chest. He felt her breath hot against him and then he jumped at the startling sensation of tiny teeth closing gently but firmly over one of his flat male nipples, using her tongue and her teeth to draw it into the same nubbin of aroused flesh that he had called from her.

Arrows of desire sizzled a path through his nerve endings from her teasing tongue straight to his groin, and he groaned, abandoning her breasts to slide his hands around her bottom and pull her higher against him. He pushed a muscled knee between her slim legs, parting them and moving steadily forward until she rode one hard thigh. She brought a hand down then, exploring him through his pants, and the feel of her small palm rubbing over his cloth-covered erection drove him wild. Holding her in place, he fumbled with his belt, roughly unzipping his pants and then stepping away from her momentarily to discard the rest of his clothing.

Elizabeth stood with her back against the bed, her chest rising and falling with her quickened breathing, her arms braced behind her on the mattress. He stepped forward again, pulling her against him, and they both made anguished sounds of frustration and delight at the feel of naked flesh against naked flesh. His hot, pulsing column pushed at the mound of her belly and when she slowly rocked back and forth, caressing him with the small motion, he closed his eyes and threw his head back, giving himself to her ministrations.

With his eyes closed, every touch of her fingers to his skin made him tremble. She smoothed her hands over his chest, flicking lightly over his nipples again, then made small circles that moved steadily lower and lower. Over his rib cage, down into the tiny well of his navel, then even lower until she was brushing the thicket of black curls that surrounded his aching hardness. She toyed with him, straying down to the creases where his thighs met his torso, stealthily sliding her fingers along those folds to the heavy sac that hung between his legs, gently cupping him in her hand with her fingers slowly slipping back and forth. But she didn't touch him as he longed for her to, and he felt himself getting harder and larger, and more and more frantic for her touch.

Finally he couldn't take another second of her sly teasing. "Touch me," he growled, dropping his head to seize her earlobe between his teeth and deliver a not-so-gentle nip of warning. He slid his own hands down her body to her hips and held her firmly with one, while with the other he dipped boldly into the shadowed cleft between her legs, finding her hot and wet and unbelievably slick and ready.

She wrapped her fingers around his straining shaft, feeling the silky heat, running her thumb up over the tip and discovering the slipperiness already forming there. She rubbed her fingers around the broad head, then down again, clasping him in a firm hand and beginning to stroke him rhythmically.

"Like this?" she whispered.

His breath whistled in and out between his teeth in agonized pleasure. His hand between her legs pushed her thighs apart until she widened her stance, then found the humid entrance to her and pushed one long finger steadily, slowly but firmly up into the tight feminine channel. "Like that," he managed. He matched his finger's motion to the strokes of her hand, feeling the pace quicken far too fast, knowing this was going to be over in a matter of moments, but he couldn't bring himself to drag her hand away. Instead, he found himself covering her hand with his free one and showing her an even more intense rhythm, tutoring her in the hot, fierce pleasures of sensual fulfillment.

But all too soon, he began to shake uncontrollably with the effort to retain control, and he had to force himself to draw her hand away, twining her fingers with his when she made a sound of protest and reached for him again. The tip of his erect staff brushed against her belly and he groaned. He knew he didn't have much time. Withdrawing his hand from her steamy center, he grabbed her by the hips and boosted her up to perch on the edge of the high bed, placing her in a perfect position to receive him. His body was so ready for release that he groaned aloud as he clasped himself in one big hand and positioned himself for the final claiming. Then he pulled her off the edge of the bed.

She slid onto him in a deep, smooth stroke so perfect she might have been made for the moment, wrapping her legs around his hips and drawing him even more closely to her. He thrust deeply into her and she cried out as her most sensitive knot of tiny nerves banged against his pelvis.

She threw her head back and looked up at him, her eyes wide, pupils dilated with passion. "I can't...I can't—"

"Yes, you can." Scarcely able to restrain himself, but still in control enough to know that he didn't want to go without her, he pushed his hand between them and found the little bump of pouting flesh with his thumb. Her body was quivering around him and he'd barely started a steady circling when her back arched and she screamed.

Inside her, strong muscular contractions squeezed his bursting flesh, and as she shuddered and heaved in his arms, Rafe felt himself gathering into one giant sensation all centered on the hot flesh snugly ensconced within her body. His hips thrust, withdrew and thrust again, slamming against her, and she screamed with each contact of flesh against flesh. His body drew taut, sensation dancing down his back, starting deep within him and pushing his seed up and out, arching him against her again and again, bucking wildly as he emptied himself into her receptive woman's well.

Finally there was nothing left to give, nothing left to feel but satiated pleasure and drowsy exhaustion. His legs trembled; her ankles slipped from their clasp behind his back and her legs slid to the floor.

He reached behind her to the gold coverlet, pulling it back before lifting her and placing her gently on the crisp sheets. Drawing the cover up around her, he walked around the foot of the big bed to the other side and climbed in. She turned to him as she had the night before on another continent and he slipped one arm beneath her, drawing her close, conscious of how small and fragile she seemed. Her hand came up to rest on his chest and she nestled against him with one leg over his thigh; the mound of their child pushed into his side, cradled between them and he felt her give a deep sigh.

Rubbing his thumb over the silky skin of her upper arm, he turned his head and kissed the top of her head. "Tired?"

"Mmm-hmm." She snuggled closer.

It was amazing what a warm, sweet woman cuddling up to you could do...when it was the right woman. He lifted a hand and put a finger under her chin, tilting her face up to his so that he could kiss her, long and tender. "Then sleep. I'll hold you."

He woke before she did. Easing his arm out from under her head, he grinned when she grumbled and curled into a little ball next to him. Shifting himself onto one elbow, he took a moment to study her features.

She was so pretty. Her complexion was roses and cream with a light sprinkling of freckles over the bridge of her nose. Her dark lashes concealed those incredible eyes—those penetrating eyes that made him feel she could see every thought in his head.

The first night they'd met, she speared him with one look from those eyes and he'd been lost. His body had leaped with interest, but it was more than that—it was as if he'd known from the very start that she was going to be his.

And she was. Satisfaction filled him. She'd finally agreed that marriage was their best choice given the situation. Idly, he wondered what would happen if he'd met her today, in Phoenix, with no pregnancy to make marriage a necessity.

Would he still have been drawn to her so strongly? Would he have called her again? Would he even consider asking her to be his wife?

Of course. That was how it was supposed to work. Arranged marriages were ridiculous, and seemed even more so now that he understood what it was like to be anticipating marriage to the woman he loved—

The woman he loved.

My God, it had been between them the whole time. How had he not known? How had he not recognized it?

On the other hand, why would he? He hadn't grown up knowing what it felt like to be loved. He'd never allowed himself to need another person, either, like he needed her. He *needed* her. It was a frightening thought to know that his happiness depended on this one small woman lying beside him.

Shifting onto an elbow, he watched the slow rhythm of her breathing. The milky globes of her breasts were hidden beneath the arms she had folded under her chin and one leg was drawn up, hiding the soft female treasure that had welcomed him earlier. Her belly, stretched and swollen, was tilted down to rest against the bed and he wondered how much bigger she would get.

She was going to need him, too, in a very physical sense that had nothing to do with sex, he realized. For assistance as her body grew even more bulky and cumbersome, but more than that, for reassurance. He wouldn't let her doubt for a single moment that he found her desirable despite her pregnancy. The fact that she carried a child made from the two of them, from their very first, memorable meeting, only made her more precious in his eyes.

Gently, he laid his hand over her stomach, over the womb where his baby rested.

His baby. *Their* baby. For a few moments he allowed himself to dream about the child growing within her womb. What would he be like as a father? he wondered. He'd promised himself over the years that any children of his never would have to know the sting of critical words, never would cry themselves to sleep because they hadn't measured up, never would choose to spend lonely holidays at boarding school rather than go home. Hell, his kids wouldn't even go to boarding school.

He's sorry, you know, even if he can't say it. Roland's words echoed in his head.

Oh, his father couldn't have been an easy man to live with even if he had mellowed, as Roland claimed. And his mother…she'd followed her husband's lead her entire life. Rafe had sensed more than once that she'd have liked to be warmer, more demonstrative and loving with him, but she'd never disobey the Grand Duke's edict that too much coddling would spoil the boy.

Rafe's children were going to know they were loved in every way there was. If that spoiled them, then too bad. It beat rejection.

He came out of his reverie then to see Elizabeth lying quietly, sleepy emerald eyes studying his face. She reached out a hand and laid it gently on his cheek and he turned his face into her palm, pressing a whisper-light kiss there before taking the hand and bringing it to the back of his neck. Slowly he leaned over her and set his mouth on hers, kissing her with all the tenderness his newly realized love gave him. When he lifted his head, there were tears in her eyes and he knew she'd caught something of his feelings in the gentle caress.

Dinner with his family was more of a success than he'd have believed was possible before this day. But now, Rafe caught himself thinking of the legions of ancestors who had lived in this very building. It would be exciting to share that with his child someday, on a visit to his father's homeland.

On a visit... For the first time he had a moment's dissatisfaction with his life-style. His child's heritage was here, where hundreds of years had passed under his family's rule. It was a remarkable legacy...was he wrong to reject it so completely?

Flying back to Wynborough that evening, to the palace where Elizabeth was staying with her parents, he remembered what she'd been pestering him about during their trip the previous afternoon. Though talking about his childhood wasn't high on his list of favorite activities, he said abruptly, "My parents—my father in particular—had very set ideas on how to raise a little duke-to-be. I had to ride, hunt, fish, speak French, read Latin, excel at mathematics and science, study the classics, recite every rule of etiquette, know proper forms of address—you name it, my father believed I should do it."

Elizabeth put a hand over his where it rested on the wheel of the car he drove. "Your childhood must have been busy."

"Busy." He laughed, but even he could hear the pain in the sound. "I wanted to please. I can remember lying awake as a very small boy, rehearsing over and over again how to greet the King of Wynborough at my first formal presentation the next day. But when the next day came, I was so nervous that I threw up while we were waiting in line to be presented. My father was livid."

Her fingers tightened briefly on his.

"They sent me to school when I was five because my father felt I lacked proper self-discipline. It was horrible. Cold showers every morning, standing in perfect lines at all times, no extra servings at meals. For a growing boy, that alone was torture. But do you know what the worst thing was?''

He sensed rather than saw her shake her head in the dark interior of the vehicle. ''The worst thing was that soon, too soon, I preferred that hellish school to my own home. At school, hard work had rewards. At home, hard work only meant more difficult tasks and more criticism.''

He stopped speaking. There was no point in going on. She got the picture.

''Rafe...'' Her voice was soft and hesitant and when he glanced at her he could see the tracks where tears had slipped down her cheeks. ''I promise our child will never be a...a product to be perfected. Our children will be works of art, great treasures to be protected and preserved for their own unique characteristics.''

Her words moved him, and the fact that she'd said ''children'' wasn't lost on him. Reaching across the car, he wiped away the telltale moisture with the pad of his thumb and caressed her cheek before returning his hand to the wheel.

''Mother, I'll be back in five days, I promise.'' Elizabeth hugged the Queen of Wynborough. ''Plenty of time to get your wedding gown altered to fit a pregnant bride.''

''But why go at all?'' her mother asked plaintively. ''It isn't as if there's anything in Phoenix for you to do in the next two weeks.''

But there is. According to Laura, Sam Flynn is back in town. It would be wonderful if I could bring my brother home for my wedding!

But aloud all she said was, ''I have to go. I don't want to be away from Rafe so long. You make the rest of the arrangements as you see fit.'' That wasn't a lie. She *didn't* want to be away from Rafe. At all.

"We'll keep it simple," Gabriella promised. She smiled wistfully. "Although it would have been nice to throw a huge wedding for at least one of my daughters!"

Elizabeth laughed ruefully, thinking of the men who had claimed each of her sisters, the whirlwind weddings and the after-the-fact announcements. "Oh, Mother, I'm sorry. We spoiled your dreams, every single one of us."

The Queen took her daughter's face in her hands and kissed her forehead. "No, dear, you didn't. In fact, you've all fulfilled the only dream your father and I have ever had for you. You've found love."

Elizabeth looked over her shoulder at Rafe, talking with the King. "Is it that obvious?"

"What, that you adore each other?" Her mother smiled. "Only to eyes that know how to spot it."

If only it were true, Elizabeth thought as they completed their good-byes and Rafe helped her into the car. He'd begun to treat her as if he truly did care for her. She'd started to hope that maybe her marriage would be more than a one-sided love affair for the rest of her life.

The trip back to Phoenix was tiring, if uneventful. She slept much of the way on both planes while Rafe read and watched movies. When they stepped out of the car into the brilliant winter sun outside his home, Elizabeth smiled and raised her face to its warmth. "I didn't even realize I'd missed this until now. Oh, Rafe, I do love this town!"

He laughed as he walked around to the trunk to get their bags. "It's a good thing. My business is firmly established here. I'd hate to have to move it now."

Halfway up the sidewalk, she stopped and turned to him. "You'd actually consider moving if I asked you to?"

There was a moment of stillness in the dry air. Slowly Rafe set down the bags he carried. "Well," he said, "I'd prefer not to move to Wynborough unless you can't be happy anywhere else, but yes, if you really wanted me to, I'd move my business.'' He reached down and took her hands, holding them in his much larger ones as he held her eyes with his intense blue gaze. ''Don't you know I'd do anything to make you happy?''

She felt her eyes filling with tears at his tender tone, and she swallowed. ''All it takes to make me happy is you.''

Something wild and bright flared in his eyes for a moment, then he dropped her hands and gathered her into his arms. ''I might have been too stubborn to admit it, but you've owned my heart since the first time I looked across a ballroom and saw those green cat-eyes watching me.'' Dropping his head, he found her mouth with his, kissing her until she hung limp in his arms, gasping for breath with her body melded to his from breast to knee. ''Let's go inside,'' he growled against her lips, ''so I can make us both very happy.''

In the middle of the night he was awakened by an odd sensation.

Rafe came fully alert in an instant with Elizabeth still in his arms. Confused, he glanced around the shadows of the bedroom he'd soon be sharing with his wife—*his wife!*— and then he felt it again.

A tiny thudding right at the spot where the mound of Elizabeth's full stomach was pressed against his side. Shifting himself fractionally, he placed his hand on the spot, then waited impatiently. There! Again, the same motion. And now that he was watching more closely, he could see by the full moonlight streaming in the window that there was a slight but definite movement beneath the surface of her skin. *Someone in there wanting to come out,* he thought whimsically.

''Hey, you in there,'' he whispered. ''It's the middle of

the night. This is when people sleep. You might as well get that concept down right now.''

A snuffling noise told him Elizabeth had awakened. Then she giggled more loudly. ''Are you talking to the baby?''

''Yes. He's keeping me awake.''

He could see her raised eyebrows in the dim light. ''He? I'm hoping 'he' is a 'she.'''

The words jogged a memory, and without really thinking about it, he said, ''You and Roland. Am I the only one who wants a boy?''

She went still beneath his hand. So still that he'd swear she wasn't breathing. Then, in an instant, she relaxed. ''Maybe,'' she said. But there was something in her voice that bothered him.

The memory came back more clearly now and he recalled the odd phrasing that he'd been too distracted to question that day. ''Roland said it would be simpler if it was a girl. Why?''

The moment the words hit the quiet night air, he wished he could get them back. Erase them and go on, blissfully unaware. A chill crawled up his back, though he didn't know why, and he felt a slow, inexorable change imbue the very air around them with dread. Moving deliberately, he sat up and looked down at her.

''Why?'' he demanded again.

She hesitated. Pushing herself to a sitting position also, she scooted back a little, moving away from him. She linked her fingers together in her lap, looked down at them, and sighed. The sound carried a distinct note of resignation. ''Your father started to tell you, but he was interrupted. There's been a great deal of discussion in recent years, in light of Wynborough's current lack of male heirs to the crown, as to how to proceed when the time comes.''

''That's great. But it doesn't affect us.''

''Well, actually, it might.'' She moved back even farther

as if she wanted to be out of his reach. "Two months ago a new proviso to the law was enacted."

"What kind of proviso?" He had a sick feeling jittering around in his stomach, and abruptly he recalled the vehement tone in his father's voice when they'd spoken of living in Phoenix. Unable to sit for another minute, he sprang from the bed, snatching a pair of sweatpants from the bedpost and stuffing his legs into them. "I'm waiting," he barked when she didn't respond.

"A proviso to ensure that the Wyndham line continues," she said in a low voice. "Since there is no eldest son to inherit, the eldest grandson will be the one to ascend the throne when my father...isn't the king anymore."

"The eldest grandson?" he repeated cautiously.

She nodded, apprehension clearly visible. "No matter which princess is his mother, the eldest grandson will be the next king."

He was incredulous. Fury rose as he realized fully what her words meant. There was a distinct possibility that his child, were it a son, would be the heir to the throne of Wynborough. "I can't believe this!" His voice was tight with the rage erupting inside him. "You know how I feel about this whole royalty thing and now you tell me if we have a son, he might be the next *king?*"

"Rafe, I didn't *plan* this," she said, a note of pleading entering her voice. "I certainly didn't intend to get pregnant the first time we met. And I didn't intend to marry you, remember?"

"You still expect me to believe that?" He was too angry to care about the words he hurled at her. "You knew who I was at the ball that night. Our fathers didn't have as much to do with this as I'd thought, did they?"

"That's not true! I had no idea who you were—"

"Sure. And pigs fly, Princess."

"I told you my father would never arrange a marriage for me. He doesn't believe in such an archaic custom."

"Maybe not, but he didn't mind sacrificing a virgin daughter for the good of the Crown, did he?"

She gasped. Tears were swimming in her eyes and as he watched, one fat drop slipped down her cheek. And still he went on, every suspicion he'd ever harbored erupting in a raging river of fury.

"I was right all along, wasn't I? You nearly had me fooled. But now your real agenda's been exposed. If you can't be the king—which you can't, being a female—then be the next best thing. Elizabeth, the Queen Mother. And I'm the perfect catch. Heir to the Grand Duchy of Thortonburg. *If* I were to inherit the title. I bet it was one hell of a shock when you found out I'm just plain old Rafe Thorton and intend to remain that way!"

The tears were pouring down her face now. "That's not what happened!" she screamed at him. She came off the bed in a rush, dragging the sheet around her to conceal her nakedness. As if he gave a damn. "I didn't know who you were when we met. I didn't even make the connection to Thortonburg when I found your card." She was shaking with rage, and he had a sudden moment of concern for the baby she carried.

"Eliz—"

"I *loved* you," she said, dashing the tears from her cheeks with one hand. "All I ever wanted was to marry you and have a family. Here in America or any other place you chose. That stupid title doesn't appeal to me any more than it does to you," she said fiercely.

"Right. And when were you planning to share this little 'proviso' with me?" He crossed his arms over his chest. "You knew about this months ago, no doubt. These kinds of laws aren't passed overnight. Were you afraid one of your sisters was going to beat you to the prize?" His heart was pounding so hard, he could feel it hammering against his wrist where it pressed against his skin and he felt as if his head was going to explode. How could she have done this to him? *Easily. You were just the means to the end, buddy.*

"I was waiting until the baby was born to tell you," she said in answer to his original question. Her voice was flat and dull. "I knew how you'd react. But if it's a girl, there would be no reason for concern. Alexandra's already expecting her first baby and my other two sisters recently married—I have every hope that one of them will produce the heir instead of me."

"Every hope," he repeated tightly.

"Every hope," she enunciated. "But you have such a phobia about your ties to the crown that it won't really matter even if it is a girl, will it, Rafe? Even if this baby is a daughter, you're still going to be stuck with a royal connection that's only one step away from the King. And you'll blame me for that for the rest of my life. I'll never be able to change my blood to something less blue. And you know what?" She stormed across the room until she was right in his face and he could see the deep, open wound he'd torn in her heart reflected in her eyes. "I wouldn't even if I could. I love my family. They're not my enemies, and I won't pretend to be somebody I'm not, even for you." She stopped and took a deep breath that hitched twice before she regained control. "You can forget this marriage. I'm going back to Wynborough to be with people who love me the way I am."

Her words stunned him. She stomped out the door and down the hall to the other end, where the room she'd slept in before still held most of her things. He heard the door slam violently and he knew there would be no talking to her the rest of the night.

You can forget this marriage.

She couldn't back out! She'd said she would marry him. *Forget this marriage.*

He felt himself begin to shake as he fully grasped what those words meant. She wasn't going to marry him. His child would not be born legitimate. His child would be raised on a separate continent from its own father with a mother who didn't want to have anything more to do with him. But worse, much worse, was the loss of the love he'd come to depend on. She'd said she was leaving, going back to Wynborough. She was leaving him.

He hadn't anticipated that when he'd accused her of wanting his title. What woman was going to stand and let a man shout at her, accuse her of all kinds of things, scoff at her honesty?

The sick feeling in his stomach returned full-force and he had to grope for the edge of the bed. He'd been wrong. He *had* to have been. No one had schemed to push her into his arms. Otherwise, she'd never be giving up the chance at marriage. He'd half assumed, stupidly, that she was only playing hard-to-get when she'd refused him before.

But she hadn't been. He could see that now. It was so clear. All she'd wanted from him was love. Not legitimacy for her child, not a ''second-best'' title for a woman who couldn't wear the crown. Just love. She'd refused to marry him repeatedly because she'd loved him and had no hope of the feeling being returned.

He dropped his head into his hands and squeezed his skull between his palms. How blind could a man be?

Oh, God, he'd been so stupid. He'd taken her love and trampled it beneath both feet, with less than no regard for her feelings. He'd been so steeped in his own bitter memories that even after his family had made a legitimate attempt at reconciliation he was still determined to punish someone.

And he'd taken it out on Elizabeth. He'd sensed her love

for him before she'd confessed it, and he'd been so confident that her heart would be his forever that he hadn't realized how easily hearts can be broken.

He'd just ground hers into dust.

Could he repair the damage? The sick feeling told him it wouldn't be easy. But he had to try.

Rising, he walked slowly down the hall to her suite and knocked on the door. But as he'd expected, she didn't answer. He listened carefully, but she wasn't sobbing—at least, not loudly enough for him to hear. With a weariness deeper than anything he'd ever felt before, he slid down the door into a sitting position and prepared to wait. When she opened that door, he intended to be there.

No matter how long it took.

Because she was the bottom line. Elizabeth was what mattered most to him. If she wouldn't forgive him, if she didn't love him anymore, he didn't know what he'd do.

Dawn came a few hours later and he still didn't hear her. Good. She must have fallen back asleep. God knew how— he hadn't been remotely tempted to close his eyes.

By eight he was tired of sitting. She rarely ever slept this late. He straightened from the cramped position in which he'd been sitting and stood, then knocked on the door. Not hard enough to make her think he was still angry, but firmly enough that she couldn't sleep through it.

Not a peep.

Fifteen minutes later he was getting worried. She still hadn't made any sound at all and his imagination was starting to rev into overdrive, quickening his pulse and shortening his breath.

"Elizabeth! Open this door. I only want to talk to you." He paused.

No answer. Oh, God, was she hurt? Lying on the bathroom floor unconscious? Those tiles were so slippery....

"Either you open it *now* or I break it down." That was an idle threat. He'd designed the house himself. There was no way anyone could kick in one of these doors.

Keeping an ear tuned for her, he hurried to his tool closet and got a few items, then returned and began taking the door off its hinges. One way or another, she was going to talk to him.

Finally, the door came free and he set it to one side, then rushed into the room. She wasn't there. Heart pounding, he checked the adjoining bath but she wasn't there, either.

Then he noticed the French doors leading to the pool terrace. The deadbolt was unlocked as was the lock on the doorknob. As he started across the room, something white and out of place on the bed's forest-green quilt caught his eye.

Snatching up the note, he scanned its contents.

Rafe
I will contact you when the baby is born. Please inform your family of the change in plans.
              HRH Elizabeth, Princess of Wynborough.

Nine

The sunlight hurt her eyes even through the dark glasses she wore.

As the driver of the rental car she'd hired sped along the highway toward Catalina, Elizabeth wished for the tenth time that she was allowed to take a painkiller for the headache that was pounding behind her eyes.

When she extracted the sheet of paper from her purse, her hands were shaking and abruptly she clasped them together in her lap, squeezing tightly enough that her knuckles turned white. She had to get herself under control before she reached Catalina, or Sam Flynn would think she was crazy.

Sam Flynn was likely to think she was crazy, anyway. After all, how many people knocked on your door and explained that you might be a long-lost prince?

She should be more excited about this venture. It was quite likely that she would be meeting her older brother for the first time in her life in less than an hour.

But nothing seemed exciting to her after the events of last night.

She swallowed and told herself to think of something—*anything*—else. But over and over again, like a scratched CD that kept skipping back to the same spot, she heard Rafe's voice in her head: *You knew who I was at the ball that night... Heir to the Grand Duchy of Thortonburg.*

The pain battered her skull. Dear God, how could he have believed that of her? She was right to break it off. He would never be able to get past his doubts, never be able to work through the anger he still felt at his father and his family for trying to make him into something he wasn't.

She recalled the look she'd seen on the Grand Duke's face the day they'd gone to visit. Victor Thorton was a man who loved his son...a man who would have to live the rest of his life knowing he had driven away his own child with his demands and his untruths. But Rafe would never fully understand that. Because he would never choose to allow himself to believe it.

Her eyes began to sting again, though she would swear there couldn't be any more tears left to fall. Last night she'd called a taxi and quietly left the house through her terrace door as soon as she could dress. Getting over the fence around the property hadn't been as easy as it might have been normally, but she'd managed it and then checked into a motel for what was left of the night. She'd cried endlessly into a pillow and risen at dawn to stare vacantly at the television until a decent hour arrived and she could place a call to Catalina.

Sam Flynn had been noncommittal on the telephone, but he'd agreed to meet with her. So after a hasty shower she'd rented this car, complete with driver this time. She would accomplish what she and her sisters had really come to the States to do—find their brother—and then she'd go home.

To Wynborough.

Even if Wynborough didn't feel like "home" anymore, it was a better place than most to raise her child... Rafe's child. Her breath caught, and she turned the sob into a cough. She'd already alarmed the driver once when he'd looked in the mirror and seen the tears flowing down her cheeks. So now she wore the dark glasses and told herself to buck up, quit sniffling. After all, she was a princess. She had an obligation to present herself well in public.

Samuel N. Flynn was an attorney-at-law, according to the listing in the telephone book. Since it was a Tuesday morning, she'd called his office and been lucky enough to find him in.

Now, as the car pulled to a stop in front of the sign announcing Flynn's business, situated in a professional building, she stepped out and mentally closed the door on all thoughts other than the task at hand.

A receptionist sat busily working at a keyboard in the waiting room. Elizabeth announced herself simply as she had on the phone, as Elizabeth Wyndham, and the woman disappeared down a long hallway. A moment later, she reappeared and invited Elizabeth to follow her.

The attorney sat behind an enormous desk which held a small assortment of objets d'art and a larger collection of neat stacks of files in rows across the top of the desk. He rose when she entered and courteously came around the desk to shake her hand and offer her a seat as the receptionist retreated to her post.

"Miss Wyndham. A pleasure to meet you. Now tell me how I can help you with this 'urgent matter' you mentioned on the phone this morning." Sam Flynn had thick, wavy brown hair and a strong jaw with a dimple in his cheek. A good-looking man in a rough, tough way that went with the broad shoulders beneath his conventional white shirt. But it was his eyes that caught her attention. Piercing, blue and compelling, they reminded her of Rafe's eyes, and she felt her composure falter as Rafe's beloved features appeared in her mind once more.

"Ah, Mr. Flynn, thank you for seeing me on such short notice."

"Sam, please, Miss Wyndham." He leaned forward to look pointedly at her ring finger, grinning mischievously. "It *is* Miss, isn't it?"

"Um, actually, it's Princess." She was wearing an unrevealing pantsuit this morning and the handsome attorney must not have noticed her pregnancy. But she found herself completely unable to respond to his lighthearted flirtation; the comment only made her want to burst into tears again. "My father is King Phillip of Wynborough."

"Good God." Sam Flynn looked mildly thunderstruck. He assessed her expression. "You aren't kidding, are you?" Then his face sobered and he leaned back against the edge of his desk, crossing his ankles and folding muscular arms over his chest in a manner that made her fear for the seams at the shoulders of his shirt. "Now you've really got me curious. What's going on?"

"Are you the Samuel N. Flynn who was once at The Sunshine Home for Children in Hope?"

He nodded, his eyes alive with interest. "One and the same."

"What does the *N.* stand for?"

He grinned again. "No-middle-name. I was dumped at the home without a middle name and they listed it on my records the same way. Hence, my *N.*"

"Mr. Fl—Sam, you may remember that years ago I had a brother who was kidnapped as a child."

"Presumed dead." He shook his head. "I was just a baby then, but I've read about it. Must have been a horrible time for your parents."

"It was. The thing is, you are exactly the same age as my brother. Until recently we believed he was dead. But new evidence led us to The Sunshine Home, where my brother is believed to have been brought a few weeks after the kidnapping.''

"I see." Sam spoke slowly and she could see why he was a lawyer. His mind worked at top speed. "And you think there's a chance I'm your brother."

"There's a chance," she agreed.

"Nah." He unfolded his arms and boosted himself to sit on the desk, long legs dangling. "You're too gorgeous to be related to me."

"When my brother disappeared, he had dark hair and blue eyes. We know he was big for his age. He looked a great deal like pictures of my father at the same age and he probably still would today." She fumbled to open her bag and pulled out two sheets of paper, unfolding them and smoothing out the creases. She passed the first one to him. "This is a picture of my father at age thirty, the age my brother would be today."

"The age I am." Sam studied the copy. "It's possible. Although I don't see any great resemblance."

"It's hard to tell from a photograph." She studied him, thinking that he could indeed be James. So why wasn't she more excited? Wasn't this what she'd come to the States for?

You also came to the States to find the man who made love to you in a garden house.

She took a deep breath, banishing another pair of blue eyes from her mind. "Would you be willing to have some bloodwork done?"

Flynn considered. "Sure. Why not?" He passed the photo back to her. Then he snapped his fingers. "Wait a minute. Did your brother have any identifying marks? Birthmarks, scars—anything like that?"

She consulted the second sheet of paper she still held, though she knew its contents by heart. "Yes. He had a small patch of freckles clustered closely together on his upper right arm. We have been warned, though, that such a mark may have faded over the years.''

''No scars?'' Sam was watching her closely.

She shook her head. ''None that would have been large enough to have lasted. James never had any kind of surgery or stitches. He was only a year old when he was kidnapped.''

''Well, then I'm afraid you've had a wasted trip, Your Highness.'' Sam heaved his bulky body off the desk and began to drag the front of his shirt free of his pants. ''I have a surgical scar that was already healed when I was brought to the Sunshine Home, so they figured it had to have occurred at least three months before. It must have been a doozy when it happened, because they could still count the stitch marks. Twenty-one in all.''

She was horrified at the thought of a tiny baby undergoing such trauma. ''At least three months before you got to the home?'' she said, thinking aloud. ''My brother hadn't been missing that long before you both turned up at the Sunshine Home.''

She stood and examined the scar in the muscle just below his ribs, seeing that despite the age of the wound, it obviously had been a ''doozy.''

''Good heavens. Surely a doctor would remember that kind of suture on a baby so young. Have you ever pursued it?''

Sam shrugged. ''They checked it out when I was dumped, but nothing turned up. That was in the days before computers, so I imagine the search was a local kind of thing. I've never bothered,'' he added. ''Whoever left me there didn't want me. I don't need them now.''

She nodded, though she felt a small ache in her heart for the little boy whose hurt still showed. The ache expanded as it reminded her of another grown man with his own childhood hurts—*No, don't go there, Elizabeth.*

Stepping back, she gathered up the papers and began to fold them before replacing them in her purse. "Sam, I'm sorry to have wasted your time. Thank you for seeing me today."

"My pleasure, Your Highness." He extended his hand and engulfed hers in a huge bear paw, holding it gently for a moment. "Good luck finding your brother."

When she got back to the car, the driver was waiting as she'd asked. He immediately headed for her next destination, a small public airstrip where she had booked a commuter flight to Tucson and then a flight to the east coast where she would leave for the transatlantic flight to Wynborough. It wasn't the most direct route she could have taken, but there was no power on earth that could induce her to go anywhere near Phoenix, not even to transfer from one airplane to another.

At the airport it suddenly dawned on her that she had the information that she and her sisters had been waiting to confirm for so long. Hurriedly, she sought a telephone and placed a call to Mitch Colton's ranch where Laura Bishop still was staying with Mitch and Alexandra, coordinating the remaining leads on finding the prince.

"Laura? It's Elizabeth."

"Princess Elizabeth! Congratulations on your engagement." Laura Bishop sounded as sweet and delightful as ever. "I'll be seeing you soon, back in Wynborough. I can't wait for the wedding and I can't wait to meet Raphael Thorton!'"

"Laura, listen to me." Elizabeth stopped and struggled to regain control of her voice, trying desperately to hold the tears at bay. She couldn't bear to talk about the wedding nor her dashed hopes of a lifetime of love. "I found Sam Flynn. He's not the one."

"He's not…then the only one left—" Laura's voice rose in excitement "—is John Colton! Alexandra's brother-in-law!"

"Yes. Is he there? I need you to talk to him right away."

"I can't." The secretary's voice was regretful. "He's still not here. Mitch and Alexandra have left messages in several locations for him, but he hasn't contacted them as far as I know."

"Tell them to send more urgent messages. We *have* to talk to him." If she concentrated hard enough on the task of finding her long-lost brother, perhaps some of the devastating pain that pierced her heart would go away. Or at least become more bearable. "I'm heading back to Wynborough soon. Call me there if you have any new information. But be careful. I don't want my parents to learn anything about this until we know for sure."

When Rafe disembarked from the flight onto which he'd bullied his way earlier in the day, Roland stood waiting in the airport lounge, his blue eyes dark with worry.

"Rafe, sorry to greet you with bad news, but I don't think she's come here. At least not yet."

Rafe nodded stoically. "Thanks for checking."

"Father has someone looking at all the flights. If she does come home, you'll know it."

"All right." He was so disappointed, he could barely force out the words.

They began walking through the airport.

"I was sure she was in love with you," Roland said. "Was I wrong?"

"You weren't wrong." Rafe shook his head. "But I—I didn't handle it very well, I'm afraid."

"Is there any way I can help? Or would you rather I just shut up?"

Despite his bone-deep misery, Rafe had to smile at his

younger brother. "Just being here is help enough." Regret for the years he could have had with Roland coursed through him and he tossed an arm around the other man's shoulders in a quick and affectionate hug.

When they reached the chauffeured limo waiting at the exit, Rafe was surprised to see his father seated inside the car.

Before he could utter a greeting, Victor held up a hand. "I know what you're thinking."

"You do?" Rafe smiled wryly. "Good, because I'm not sure I do anymore."

"Raphael, I'm sure you think I'm being so helpful out of a desire to link my house with the Wyndhams'." He grimaced. "And I admit, there's a part of me that would like that very much. But that's not why I'm here. In fact, I'll leave if you'd prefer I not involve myself in your life."

It was a shock to see that his father's intent blue eyes were the same ones that stared back at him every morning. Quietly, he said, "I believe you have my best interests at heart, Father. And that's good enough for me." And he realized it was true.

The moisture that gleamed in the older man's eyes embarrassed them both, and there was silence in the car for a moment.

The Grand Duke inclined his head. "I never should have tried to force you into a marriage based on—"

"Lies?" asked Rafe.

"Half truths, at the very least." The older man cleared his throat. "I know what it's like to love someone. And it was clear when we saw you together that you and Elizabeth were very much in love. Being my son, it's entirely possibly that you've done something unforgivably stupid—"

Both his sons laughed and the tension in the vehicle dissipated.

Then Rafe sobered. "I hope it's not unforgivable."

Slowly, hesitantly, his father reached over and laid a comforting hand on his son's knee. "We'll do whatever we can to help you make it right."

Several hours later, a servant knocked on the door of the smoking room where Rafe, his father and his brother were closeted.

The Grand Duke bellowed, "Enter," and Trumble came into the room, carrying a single sheet of paper on a silver tray.

"A telephone message for you, Your Grace."

Victor practically leaped on the man. "Well, give it here! What does it say?" The paper slipped from his grasp and fluttered toward the floor, but before it could land Roland had snatched it up again.

"The Princess has arrived at the palace," he announced. Then he cleared his throat. "She, ah, visited a man, an American attorney named Samuel Flynn in Catalina, Arizona, before leaving the States." He looked questioningly at Rafe. "Friend of yours?"

Rafe shook his head. "Apparently a friend of *hers*," he said in a grim tone.

"Will she see you if you call on her?" asked his father.

"Not a chance." Once he would have endured torture rather than admit to his father that he'd made a mistake. Today, it no longer seemed to matter.

"Well, then, we'll have to get you in without being announced."

Two hours later, Victor's limousine was pulling up to the guardhouse at the palace gates.

"The Grand Duke of Thortonburg and my son Roland, Prince of Thortonburg," he announced imperiously to the guard as the man checked the two men seated in the rear interior of the vehicle.

The guard punched some buttons on the face of a cell

phone and received permission to admit them. As the gates slowly opened, and the limo rolled into the lush green gardens that led to the palace, Roland eyed the back of their chauffeur's head and chuckled. "Very good, Father. Very good."

The chauffeur glanced over his shoulder, blue eyes gleaming. "Thank you, Father."

In the end, it was even simpler than Rafe had anticipated. Roland and the Grand Duke left him along a deeply wooded riding path close to the inner edge of the estate. Striding along the path, Rafe looked around to get his bearings. He'd chosen this location because he knew the woods grew up to the edge of the gardens near here. The guards around the palace grounds generally stayed within sight but not necessarily within hearing of the royal family. With that in mind, he hoped to get close enough to the house so that when Elizabeth came out for a stroll, he could speak to her even if he had to sit out here all night.

He couldn't believe how easy it had been, considering the King's well-known fetish for security. But the Grand Duke would never be expected to be a threat. And since the King's own security team had personally approved any chauffeurs entering any premises where the royal family was in residence, the man driving the Grand Duke's own limo had been cleared when his uniform insignia identified him as someone previously checked out.

To his right Rafe could see the beginning of a small clearing. As he got a better look, he muttered, "I'll be damned."

The palace grounds were enormous and he wasn't at all familiar with them. The sight of a glass-walled gazebo in the middle of the clearing made him shake his head wryly. Could it be the same one? It looked exactly like the one engraved in his memories—surely there couldn't be another so similar?

The drop of rain that hit his left cheek surprised him, so immersed in his surveillance was he. But as the drops quickly became a deluge, he sprinted for the only available cover, the little glass gazebo where he'd made love to Elizabeth the very first time.

Only moments after he rushed through the little entrance into the dry interior, a noise had him whirling to look for a pursuer. Elizabeth halted halfway through the door, her hand to her throat in a gesture of shock that matched the expression on her face.

"Rafe!"

He'd recovered his wits while she goggled at him, though her appearance was as much a surprise to him. "Why don't you come in before you get soaked?"

"I—" She glanced behind her at the downpour. "What are you doing here?"

"Coming after you."

She straightened, and he could see her regaining her composure. She wore jeans and an oversize sweater, but when she moved into the room, her manner was so regal that she might as well have had on a crown. "You've wasted a trip." The words dripped ice.

"Why did you come in here?"

Her eyelids flickered. "I was out for a walk and when it started to rain, I simply ran for the nearest cover. I *didn't* come here for any other reason."

He might have said something at that, but a man getting ready to beg for his life was smart not to antagonize the woman he wanted to share it with.

Again, she questioned him. "Why did you come here?"

"I can't forget it."

She blinked, looked at him through cool green eyes. "I beg your pardon?"

"Back in Phoenix you told me to forget about marriage. I can't."

"*That's* what you wormed your way in here to tell me? How did you get in here, anyway?" She held up a hand. "Never mind." Turning, she looked through the glass panes of the gazebo window. "Go away."

Her back was rigid, her arms hugged closely together over the swell of the baby. He could see her in profile, her lips pressed tightly together and her chin trembling.

"I've made peace with my father," he said softly.

"That's nice." She didn't look at him, but her tone wasn't quite so belligerent.

There was another awkward silence while he tried to think of something brilliant that would persuade her to give him another chance. Finally he just blurted out the words that were reverberating in his mind. "You said you loved me."

She flinched. Lifting a hand, she placed it against the condensation on the window. When she removed it, her small handprint was visible. But it was so humid in the garden house that even as they watched, the outline began to fade. "Some things aren't meant to be permanent," she said sadly.

"Elizabeth…" Was there no way to reach her? "If you don't want to get married, we don't have to. We can live together for the rest of our lives without making it legal. Just please—" His voice cracked. Stopping for a moment, he closed the space between them and stood directly behind her. "Elizabeth, I don't want to live without you. Please come back to me."

She didn't respond, but she didn't rebuff him, either. Raising his hands, he nearly placed them lightly on her shoulders but after a moment he let them drop. "Please," he repeated. "Give me another chance. I was wrong about everything. Your father, my father, you—"

"You would live with me even if I refused to marry you? Why? So you can hound me to death until I agree to make your child legal?" The words were lightly mocking, but he heard the pain underlying them, and his heart sank.

Quietly he said, "Some of us learn lessons more slowly than others. It took me far too long to learn mine."

He took a deep breath. "I love you."

Her emerald eyes widened and he could see the flare of an emotion she couldn't hide.

"I love you," he said again, pressing his advantage. "I should have told you before. I should have trusted you—"

She put a hand over his lips. "It's all right, Rafe. We'll make it all right now." She cradled his face in her hands and lifted herself on tiptoe against him.

Rafe gathered her closer and fit his mouth to hers, sweet relief flowing through him. Despite everything, she'd forgiven him. Could she ever understand how much he loved her? His mouth grew more demanding as he dragged her close, his body urging him to demonstrate his need for her.

Her hand smoothed over his shoulder and slipped around to the back of his neck as her tongue began to dance with his and her body softened and melted against him. In seconds the kiss heated into a flashfire that threatened to rage out of control.

The only thing that saved him from dragging her to the floor where they stood was the moisture on his face.

No, on *her* face.

The little annoyance crept into his consciousness, interrupting the intensity of the kiss, and he tore his mouth away from hers so he could wipe the rain from their faces. Only it wasn't rain.

Elizabeth was crying.

He gentled his hands on her, slipping his palms up to cradle her jaw. "What's wrong, Princess? Is it me?"

"N-no." She shook her head. Her eyes were as green as

spring grass, wet as the windowpanes around them, and tears continued to flow down her cheeks. She brought her hands up to cover his.

"I'll retain the title," he said desperately. Though it wasn't the path he'd intended his life to take, he'd do it in a minute if she'd agree to stay. To his shock, the words didn't bother him as once they would have.

But she shook her head again. "It's not the title. I'll love you no matter what you want to do with your life."

As the impact of what she was saying sank in, he felt the fist squeezing his heart begin to loosen its grip. He let his hands slide down from her face, turning them to take hers in a gentle clasp as he kissed her gently. "So if there's no problem, why are you crying?"

"I'm crying because I'm so happy." She leaned toward him for another kiss.

But at the last moment, he remembered something. "Just who in the hell," he said, holding his mouth a breath above hers, "is Samuel Flynn of Catalina, Arizona?"

"Who do you think he is?" Though she didn't withdraw, there was a sudden still quality about her that told him what she feared.

"I don't believe you're involved with him, because you love *me*."

She laughed, her face lightening and her body relaxing again. "So modest."

"But he's someone very important. He's the 'other matter' you came to Phoenix about, isn't he?"

She nodded. "There's reason to believe my brother James survived the kidnapping."

"What?" He was thunderstruck. Feeling the mound of their child pressed against him, he could appreciate for the first time the hell the King and Queen must have gone through and the thought made him nearly ill.

"It's true," she confirmed. "He almost certainly survived. We traced him to an orphans' home in Arizona and narrowed our search to three men. Sam Flynn was the second.''

''And—?''

''He isn't my brother. He has a scar to prove it. Which means that the third man probably is the heir to the throne. My sisters are waiting for him to return home so we can speak with him.''

''My God! Your parents will be so—wait a minute. *That's* why you weren't quite as concerned about this new law, isn't it?'' Remorse struck him anew for the horrible words he'd thrown at her.

She hesitated. ''Until James is found, the first male heir *could* well be the Crown Prince. I am worried, but I also know my chances are as good of having a female child. If it's a son and we don't want him to be king, it could be done, but it would be a tedious process. As a last resort, we can petition the parliament to pass over him.''

Rafe gathered her into his arms. ''We'll deal with it together when the time comes, *if* the time comes. And if your brother is found, then we can just be an average pair of doting parents.''

She smiled. ''Well, perhaps not quite average.''

''The important thing,'' he said, drawing her even nearer, ''is that we spend the rest of our lives together.''

And as he found her lips and claimed his princess, he felt something inside him click into place, something he'd waited for his whole life. He was loved.

Epilogue

Elizabeth stood at the back of Wynton Chapel, her sisters gathered around her.

Alexandra, ever practical, had a list in her hand. "Now, Serena, don't forget to hand your flowers to Katherine right before they go up to the altar. She'll hand them to me. When Elizabeth hands you her bouquet, you two repeat the same thing so your hands are free to help with her train—" She broke off, fishing a tissue from her bodice to dab at her upper lip.

"Are you all right?" Katherine stopped adjusting Elizabeth's bridal veil and took her eldest sister by the elbow. "I thought this morning sickness stuff was only for the first three months."

"The doctor swears it will ease any day now," Alexandra replied, taking deep, shaky breaths. "If he's wrong, I'm going to have him beheaded."

"All you have to do is make it through the wedding," Serena said. "Then you can throw up all you want."

"Thanks," said Alexandra dryly.

"The *wedding*," Serena repeated. "I'm so glad at least one of us is getting married here. The rest of us will live vicariously through you, Elizabeth."

"And it will make Mummy and Daddy so happy." Katherine's face lost a bit of its happy glow. "I still feel badly that I deprived them of the chance to throw us a big 'do.'"

"Mummy and Daddy are happy for all of us," Elizabeth reassured them all, thinking back to her mother's words before she'd left for Phoenix the last time. "They wanted each of us to find love and hold it tight for the rest of our lives. And we have."

"I only wish we could have found James," Alexandra said. "What a wedding present that would have been!"

There was a moment of silence as they contemplated how very close they might be to giving their parents the gift of a lifetime.

"One last group hug," Serena said as she sniffed and dabbed at a tear. "The music's started and we have to start down the aisle any minute."

The four sisters huddled together, Katherine fussing at them not to wrinkle Elizabeth's gown.

She loved them so much, Elizabeth thought, swallowing tears of her own. It was almost inconceivable to think that they'd set out for the States mere months ago. So many events had occurred that it seemed much longer.

And now they would all be married. The wedding would barely be over before preparations for the coronation anniversary celebration would move into high gear. Mitch and Alexandra, along with Katherine and her new husband, Trey, as well as Serena and Gabe, would be staying in Wynborough until after the festivities.

Her smile faded a bit. The only person missing was Laura, whom they all cared for dearly. But she was needed at the Colton ranch in case John Colton showed up during Mitch's absence.

The wedding coordinator hissed at them then, and a maid handed Katherine her flowers. Katherine blew Elizabeth a kiss as she started up the aisle, and Alexandra gave her a sickly smile when her turn came. Serena accepted her bridesmaid's bouquet and flashed her one last wink before moving toward the front of the enormous old church.

Then it was her turn. King Phillip, who had been watching his other three daughters, came to her side and offered her his arm. One single tear slipped down his cheek and she reached up and wiped it away with her thumb.

"Don't *you* start," she said. "Serena was bad enough. I refuse to get married with smudged mascara."

Her father's chuckle was genuine. "Sorry. I was remembering you as a bare-bottomed baby and it suddenly hit me that very soon you'll have a baby of your own."

She grimaced. "I did things a bit out of order."

"It doesn't matter." Her father's tone was fierce, but his eyes softened as he looked toward the front of the chapel where the woman he'd loved for more than thirty years waited to see him give away their child. "What matters is that you and Rafe love each other, and for that, your mother and I are very, very thankful—for all four of our daughters' marriages. Not everyone is so lucky."

"We had a fine example to show us what it should be like." She gave him one last, misty smile. "I love you, Daddy."

He led her forward then. As she got near enough to the front of the church to see the tall, broad-shouldered man waiting there with his father and brother and a line of other attendants, she gave Rafe a radiant smile.

Her father was right. They *were* lucky.

And she intended to show Rafe every day for the rest of their lives just how much she valued his love.

Turn the page for a sneak preview
of the next magnificent ROYALLY WED *title,*

MAN...MERCENARY...MONARCH

by top-notch talent Joan Elliott Pickart,
on sale in February 2000
in Silhouette Special Edition.

——

Fingers of sunlight inched beneath the curtains to tiptoe across Laura Bishop's face, waking her. She opened her eyes slowly, then in the next instant sat bolt upright on the bed, her heart racing as she realized she had absolutely no idea where she was.

The cobwebs of sleep disappeared with a blink, to be replaced by vivid images of the previous night...and John.

She glanced around the small motel room, then saw a scrap of paper on one of the bed pillows. She snatched it up, and read aloud the message written in a bold, sprawling handwriting.

"Laura,
   I hope you find your rainbow. You deserve it.
   John"

Laura sank back against the pillows and reread the note. John, her mind whispered. They'd only exchanged first names, but they'd shared so much. He remembered what she'd said about wishing to find the rainbow that would bring her the true happiness she was seeking. She had spoken and he had listened.

John, her man of the magical night. He was so magnificent, strong yet gentle, so sensitive and caring.

John, who was facing the tremendous challenge of raising a son he hadn't even known he had. He'd trusted her enough to share his fears with her, his feelings of inadequacy regarding his new, daunting and awe-evoking role.

John. Their lovemaking had been so exquisitely beautiful, it was beyond description. Magic. In the world they'd created together, every touch and kiss had been ecstasy. They had moved as one, a single entity, their dance of love so synchronized and perfect, it was as though they'd been lovers for years.

"John," Laura whispered, then sighed.

She had no regrets about her rash, out-of-character actions of last night. None. The only shadow hovering over her was the realization that she would never see John again. She'd known that at the onset, but still...

No, no, she had to be sophisticated and mature about this. Facts were facts. And memories were memories, hers to keep.

"Goodbye, John," Laura said softly as she clutched the note. "Thank you."

She showered and dressed, then after one last look at the room, closed the door behind her with a quiet click. She turned, blinked away sudden and unwelcome tears, lifted her chin and prepared to drive back to the Colton ranch.

Alone.

During the fifteen miles she had to cover to reach the Rocking C Ranch, Laura gave herself a continuous stern lecture.

Before she entered the house, she decreed, she would have pushed the memories of her lover to a safe corner of her mind.

The long hours she spent in that house waiting to fulfill her assignment were difficult enough without aching for the sight, the sound, the taste and touch of a man she would never see again.

Laura peered into the kitchen, breathed a sigh of relief when she saw it was empty, then headed for the pot of prepared coffee. She settled at the big oak table with a mug of the steaming brew.

And thought about John.

She jerked in her chair as Betty, the Colton housekeeper, entered the kitchen from the mudroom beyond. She was carrying a basket of eggs and went to the sink to rinse them. "Sleep well?"

"Oh, I...you bet," Laura said, feeling a warm flush creep onto her cheeks.

"Is everything okay?" Betty said, glancing over at her, then resuming her chore.

"I'm just dreading facing another long day, I guess," Laura said. "I've only been here alone for a week, and it seems like a year. The thing is, I have no idea how many more days there will be. Heaven only knows when John Colton will decide to make a trip home for a visit. I have to sit here and wait until he shows up."

"Well, there's worse places to be than the Colton ranch." Betty paused and shook her head. "I still find it hard to believe that our John might actually be Prince James of Wynborough. When the Coltons adopted him as a baby, there wasn't a clue about his identity. John is in for a mighty big shock when he does come home."

"I should have asked you this before, Betty. How do you think John will feel about this news?"

"No telling," Betty said, shutting off the water in the sink. "John is impossible to predict. He's a Colton, but he never has thought or acted like one."

"Well, he really isn't a Colton. He's a Wyndham."

"As far as his parents and his brother, Mitch, are concerned, he's a Colton," Betty said decisively. "They love him as their own. That will never change, no matter what new fancy name and title John has. A prince. Good gracious, wonders never cease."

"A prince who was kidnapped as an infant and believed to be dead all these years," Laura said. "And I'm the one who has been assigned the nifty task of explaining his true identity to him. I hope he doesn't get into a kill-the-messenger state of mind."

"Now there's a thought," Betty said with a burst of laughter. "Well, I'll see you later. Oh, and, Laura? The next time you stay out all night, turn off your bedroom light before you leave, would you?"

"Oh, good grief." Laura plunked one elbow on the table and rested her forehead in her hand. "How embarrassing."

"There's no shame in being a healthy young woman with wants and needs. I just couldn't resist taking a poke at you. I'll see you when I get back."

"Bye," Laura mumbled.

A heavy silence fell over the room, and Laura drained her coffee mug quickly, wishing to escape from the sudden chill of loneliness that seemed to have dropped over her like a dark cloud.

She spent the next hour writing letters to her parents, her sister, her best friend. But in none of the letters was there one word about her magical night with John.

No, she thought, placing the stamp on the third envelope, those memories were hers alone. She'd keep them tucked safely in her heart for all time.

A sharp knock sounded at the front door, and Laura jerked at the sudden noise. She hadn't heard a vehicle approach the house. Maybe it was one of the ranchhands looking for Betty.

She got to her feet and opened the door with a pleasant expression on her face.

Then she stopped breathing as a gasp caught in her throat.

Standing before her, with a blanket-covered bundle nestled to his shoulder, was John.

John, her mind hammered in disbelief. Her man of the magical night. Magnificent, tall, powerful, sensitive, compelling John was staring right at her with a shocked expression in his face.

Dear heaven, how had he found her? What was he doing here?

The answer suddenly became painfully obvious.

Her lover was John Colton.

The long-lost Prince James of Wynborough...

Don't miss Silhouette's newest cross-line promotion,

Four royal sisters find their own Prince Charmings as they embark on separate journeys to find their missing brother, the Crown Prince!

Royally Wed

The search begins in October 1999 and continues through February 2000:

On sale October 1999: **A ROYAL BABY ON THE WAY** by award-winning author **Susan Mallery** (Special Edition)

On sale November 1999: **UNDERCOVER PRINCESS** by bestselling author **Suzanne Brockmann** (Intimate Moments)

On sale December 1999: **THE PRINCESS'S WHITE KNIGHT** by popular author **Carla Cassidy** (Romance)

On sale January 2000: **THE PREGNANT PRINCESS** by rising star **Anne Marie Winston** (Desire)

On sale February 2000: **MAN...MERCENARY...MONARCH** by top-notch talent **Joan Elliott Pickart** (Special Edition)

ROYALLY WED
Only in—
SILHOUETTE BOOKS

Available at your favorite retail outlet.

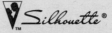

If you enjoyed what you just read,
then we've got an offer you can't resist!

Take 2 bestselling
love stories FREE!

Plus get a FREE surprise gift!

Clip this page and mail it to Silhouette Reader Service™

IN U.S.A.	IN CANADA
3010 Walden Ave.	P.O. Box 609
P.O. Box 1867	Fort Erie, Ontario
Buffalo, N.Y. 14240-1867	L2A 5X3

YES! Please send me 2 free Silhouette Desire® novels and my free surprise gift. Then send me 6 brand-new novels every month, which I will receive months before they're available in stores. In the U.S.A., bill me at the bargain price of $3.12 plus 25¢ delivery per book and applicable sales tax, if any*. In Canada, bill me at the bargain price of $3.49 plus 25¢ delivery per book and applicable taxes**. That's the complete price and a savings of over 10% off the cover prices—what a great deal! I understand that accepting the 2 free books and gift places me under no obligation ever to buy any books. I can always return a shipment and cancel at any time. Even if I never buy another book from Silhouette, the 2 free books and gift are mine to keep forever. So why not take us up on our invitation. You'll be glad you did!

225 SEN CNFA
326 SEN CNFC

Name	(PLEASE PRINT)	
Address	Apt.#	
City	State/Prov.	Zip/Postal Code

* Terms and prices subject to change without notice. Sales tax applicable in N.Y.
** Canadian residents will be charged applicable provincial taxes and GST.
  All orders subject to approval. Offer limited to one per household.
  ® are registered trademarks of Harlequin Enterprises Limited.

©1998 Harlequin Enterprises Limited

Desire®

These women are about to find out what happens when they are forced to wed the men of their dreams in **Silhouette Desire's** new series promotion:

The Bridal Bid

Look for the bidding to begin in **December 1999** with:

GOING...GOING...WED! (SD #1265)
by **Amy J. Fetzer**

And look for
THE COWBOY TAKES A BRIDE (SD#1271)
by **Cathleen Galitz** in **January 2000:**

Don't miss the next book in this series,
MARRIAGE FOR SALE (SD #1284)
by **Carol Devine**, coming in **April 2000.**

The Bridal Bid only from **Silhouette Desire**.

Available at your favorite retail outlet.

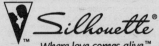

Silhouette®
Where love comes alive™

ENTER FOR
A CHANCE TO WIN*
Silhouette's 20th Anniversary Contest

Tell Us Where in the World
You Would Like *Your* Love To Come Alive...
And We'll Send the Lucky Winner There!

Silhouette wants to take you wherever
your happy ending can come true.

Here's how to enter: Tell us, in 100 words or less,
where you want to go to make your love come alive!

In addition to the grand prize, there will be 200
runner-up prizes, collector's-edition book sets
autographed by one of the Silhouette anniversary
authors: **Nora Roberts, Diana Palmer,
Linda Howard** or **Annette Broadrick**.

DON'T MISS YOUR CHANCE TO WIN!
ENTER NOW! No Purchase Necessary

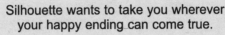

Silhouette®
Where love comes alive™

Name:

Address:

City: State/Province:

Zip/Postal Code:

Mail to Harlequin Books: **In the U.S.**: P.O. Box 9069, Buffalo, NY
14269-9069; **In Canada**: P.O. Box 637, Fort Erie, Ontario, L4A 5X3